The Mist Lizard

© Marc Alexander

ISBN 978-1-909473-13-3

Text prepared by www.willowebooks.org.uk

The Mist Lizard

by

Marc Alexander

Published by Willow Books

For Jem Alexander

For Jenn Alexander

1 The Forbidden Mountain

'You mustn't go up there – it's *tapu*!' Mani declared. Roger Hepworth looked at the anxious face of the Maori boy, then let his gaze travel up the mountain. Its peak was bald and scarred with outcrops of rock, but the lower slopes were carpeted with dark New Zealand bush. There was something menacing about the sombre evergreen trees, so silent and still in the hot sunlight, that Roger felt he hardly needed to ask the question:

'What is *tapu*, Mani?'

'Yes, why can't we explore it?' demanded his cousin, Susan. Mani shrugged and shuffled his bare feet in the lush grass.

'It's a bad place to go,' he said reluctantly. He felt that these two young *pakehas* – *pakehas* being the Maori name for white persons – who had only just arrived from England, would laugh at him if he explained fully. He tried to change the subject, saying: 'Let's go down to the creek, maybe well catch some crays.'

'But what does the word mean?' Roger persisted. He was a tall, thin boy of fourteen with long fair hair and light blue eyes. Mani Potaka was of the same age. He lived in the Maori township which stood nearby on the bank of the river that curved round the foothills of the Awapuni Ranges.

'*Tapu* is *tapu*' he retorted. 'I don't know the English word for it, but it's a place you can't go. Maybe you'd call it evil.'

'Are there spirits and things?' Susan asked. She was a contrast to her cousin Roger. Six months older, she had almost blue-black hair and grey eyes which, her father had told her, were the result of her mother's Irish blood.

'If you're afraid we'll go up by ourselves tomorrow,' Roger said. 'I'll bet your old spirits won't bother us.'

'I'm not afraid,' Mani protested. 'But I'm not stupid, either. You go up tomorrow, you smart *pakehas*, and I won't care if the Mist Lizard gets you.' He turned and ran off towards his village.

'Now you've upset him,' Susan scolded. 'You're a mean pig, especially when he's been so kind, showing us around while Daddy's been busy.'

'I didn't mean to hurt his feelings,' Roger said. 'I just thought I'd get him to tell us what's so strange about the mountain.'

'That's no excuse. You only think of what you want. You must admit you're rather selfish . . .' She turned, swinging her black hair, and followed the track which wound in the direction of the sheep station where the children were staying.

Roger sighed. It was a pity, he thought, that he and his cousin so often exchanged hard words. Of course he hadn't meant to hurt Mani's feelings, but he was fascinated by the mountain. And what was it the Maori boy had said about a 'mist lizard'?

He was dawdling along the track when the oppressive silence of the forest – so different to the English woods he was used to – was shattered by the clatter of a helicopter. Susan looked over her shoulder and called to him, 'Hurry up, that's Daddy coming back. He may have some pictures of the stele.'

Their brief quarrel forgotten, the pair raced in the direction of the sound. They reached the brow of the slope and saw below them the large wooden one-storey house and the collection of white farm buildings which made up the Ronson sheep station. A yellow helicopter stood on

2

the rose-bordered lawn. Its door opened and a burly, bearded passenger climbed out bent double because the rotor still swished above his head.

'Was it worth coming twelve thousand miles to see?' asked Susan, running towards him.

'Was it worth it!' her father laughed, picking her up and whirling her round as he had done when she was much smaller. 'It certainly was. It's the most exciting find I've ever seen.'

Dusk was falling over the Awapuni Ranges and, with supper over, a group of people sat on the farmhouse verandah. Mrs Ronson, the wife of Bill Ronson the station owner, lit two softly hissing pressure lamps around which hundreds of moths swirled madly.

'Uncle, please tell us all about it,' Roger said. In the soft light Professor Simon White held his digital camera and the others on the verandah craned forward to see the screen. Apart from the children and the Reasons, there was Scott Baker, the deer-hunting helicopter pilot; a young Maori teacher who ran the one-man school in the nearby township, and three station shepherds. They looked like American cowboys without guns, and always seemed to be cracking jokes against each other. In the shadows sat an old man with a wrinkled face and a snowy beard which flowed over his patched waistcoat. The others called him Ol' Gully, and he called himself 'the last of the old-time prospectors'.

'I'd better begin at the beginning,' Professor White said. 'As you know Mr Gully made the find a couple of months ago. It was a stele – or stone pillar – with intricate carvings on it Now what was remarkable was that the Maori people were, and still are, marvellous wood-carvers but, because they did not have metal tools, they did not carve stone in the same way. So when the stele was discovered it immediately raised the questions – who had carved it, how old was it and what did its hieroglyphics

3

mean?'

'Do you mean it may not be Maori work at all?' asked Roger.

'I think it was there long before the Maoris came to New Zealand a thousand years ago,' the Professor replied. 'It appears to be amazingly ancient. Because of the work I'd done on inscriptions in the Middle East and South America the authorities invited me to come and study it I saw it for the first time today and took these photographs.' He passed round the camera which showed a picture of a short column of stone surrounded by ferns.

While it was being discussed Roger remembered the thrill he had felt when his famous uncle had invited him to come on this trip to New Zealand, he knew one of the reasons was that Susan needed companionship because her mother and father had separated recently. Unhappily, they had had widely different interests, Simon White spending most of his time abroad on archaeological work while all Mrs White had wanted was a normal home life.

Susan had hardly mentioned it on the long flight to Auckland, but Roger sensed that while she was pleased to be with her father, she was still deeply upset over the break-up. Perhaps it was this which made her inclined to quarrel with him.

She had cheered up a lot after they had travelled to the Awapuni Ranges lying to the south-east of huge Lake Taupo. They had then made the final part of the journey in a hired Land Rover to the remote sheep station where they had been welcomed by kindly Bill Ronson and his wife. On the first day of their visit they had made friends with Mani, whose father – a champion sheep shearer – worked on the station. The boy had shown them the tiny township where he lived and had taken them swimming in a safe part of the river. Meanwhile the Professor had prepared his equipment and waited for the arrival of the helicopter

4

which would take him to the site of the stele on the other side of the mountain which dominated the landscape, the mountain which the children wanted to explore.

That morning the helicopter had arrived. It belonged to Scott Baker, a licensed deer-culler – or hunter – whose job it was to control the deer population which lived in the bush. At first Susan had been horrified when she saw several deer carcasses hanging from the light machine. The culler explained that since deer had been introduced into New Zealand they had multiplied in such numbers they were endangering the bush – and its wildlife – by eating the young trees.

'Sometimes you are forced to be cruel to be kind,' he had explained, but Susan had still looked doubtful. Roger had been more interested in the high-powered rifle with telescopic sights which rested on the passenger seat.

Now, as he looked at the picture of the stone which was responsible for bringing him on this adventure, he was reminded of the runic carvings of the Norsemen. He had read many books on archaeology because he wanted to take up the same career as his uncle, and he dreamed of someday finding a treasure-filled tomb like that of Tutankhamun.

'Could a Viking ship have come here before the Maoris, arrived?' he suggested.

'I doubt it,' the professor answered. 'The Vikings may have been the first to reach America, but even for them New Zealand would have been too far. It reminds me a bit of a carving I once saw at Lake Titicaca in Peru, but as yet I can't make anything of it.'

'It couldn't be a hoax, like the Piltdown skull?' Susan asked. Her father shook his mane of grey hair under which his face looked surprisingly young.

'I don't think so. The weathering of the stone could not be faked, but I'll be able to tell when I go back and study it thoroughly,'

'The bush round it is so thick I was lucky to find a clearing nearby,' said the helicopter pilot 'No wonder it wasn't found until Ol' Gully came on it. The Maoris would never have come across it – right, old mate?'

That's right,' the prospector chuckled from the shadows. 'They wouldn't have gone within miles of it'

'Why not?' Roger asked.

The school teacher pointed to where the bulk of the mountain was silhouetted against the moonrise.

'That mountain is *tapu*,' he explained. 'And the carving is on the slopes behind it.'

Roger caught Susan's eye, then asked: 'Will someone please tell us what *tapu* means?'

'It's Maori bad luck,' said one of the shepherds. 'Like a curse or something that can bring disaster to those who break it'

'To my people *tapu* means sacred,' explained the teacher. 'It can apply to a place or a thing. The most famous object to have *tapu* is Korotangi, which is a bird carved from stone and which somehow reached New Zealand from Asia long before Captain Cook came. In the old days certain trees or rocks were declared by the *tohungas* – or priests – to be *tapu* because they belonged to forest spirits. Burial grounds were *tapu*, too, and if the law of *tapu* was not respected the Maoris believed the results were terrible. It could even mean death.'

'Yeah, that's right,' chimed in a shepherd known as Bluey because of his red hair. 'A couple of years back a new road was being put through a valley near here and a young Maori bloke drove a bulldozer right through an old cemetery. 'Course he didn't know it was there because he'd come from a different part of the country, but when he found out what he'd done he fell sick. He seemed to be pretty crook but the hospital doctors couldn't find anything physically wrong with him. The poor joker knew he was going to die because he'd broken *tapu*, and sure

6

enough he did before the month was out'

'Why is this particular mountain *tapu*?' Roger asked.

'I reckon because there's greenstone – that's New Zealand jade – up there and the *tohungas* – the old Maori priests – wanted to keep it for themselves,' said Gully. 'I was after greenstone when I found that carving. Made me famous, it did. Got me picture in the paper – anyone want to see it?'

From the pocket of his grubby jacket he took out a well-creased newspaper cutting.

'You've shown us that a dozen times,' groaned Bluey. 'Why don't you send it to Hollywood and you might get a part in a Frankenstein film'

'You shepherd blokes are all the same,' the old man grumbled. 'You get as silly as your sheep.'

'It was not because of greenstone,' said the teacher quietly. 'The mountain is *tapu* because of the Mist Lizard.'

'I've never heard of that,' Bill Ronson said, 'and I've been here ten years.'

'That's because you are not a Maori, Mr Ronson,' the teacher laughed. 'The Mist Lizard is a mythical creature which, in the old days, was believed to haunt the upper part of the mountain.'

'Something like the Abominable Snowman?' Susan asked.

'More like a Pink Elephant,' Bluey chuckled.

'I'm going to turn in,' said the Professor, climbing to his feet. 'Scott is taking me back to the stele early in the morning. I'm going to camp there a few days to make some tests.'

'Why can't we come?' Susan demanded.

'There's not enough room for all of you in the chopper,' said Scott. I'd ferry you out one after another only I have to go straight to the west ranges. When my work lets up I'll take you to see it'

'You'll have more fun with Mani,' added the Professor. 'I'll only be digging to see if I can find any artefacts which may give me a clue.'

'Bed for me, too,' said Bill Ronson. 'Got to make an early start.' He turned to the shepherds. 'I want to repair that fence at the north end of the Hundred Acre Paddock,' The men nodded, said goodnight and walked off to their sleeping quarters. Roger leaned on the verandah rail while Mrs Ronson took the kerosene lamps inside. He gazed up at the sky where the moon was now riding in a sea of tattered cloud above the summit of the *tapu* mountain.

As he watched it seemed that the clouds above the peak took on a strange shape and Roger felt he understood how the Maoris could believe there was something eerie up there.

'*Tapu* or not,' he muttered, 'I'm going to climb you.'

2 Tyrannosaurus Rex

The track Roger and Susan had been following became a tunnel of dim green. Sunlight only reached it after filtering through the dense foliage of bush trees and tangles of creepers. Huge ferns bordered the path, their graceful fronds often meeting overhead. The air was hot and still, smelling of earth which had never been disturbed by man and the only sound was the clear call of a bellbird.

'It's getting steep,' Susan panted.

'Yes, and it looks as though the track is going to run out soon,' her cousin said. 'We'll have to find our way through the bush like real explorers. Uncle told me that there are still tracts of land in New Zealand no one has ever visited. Wouldn't it be fantastic if we were the first to set foot here.'

'We'd better be careful not to get lost,' said Susan. 'Mr Ronson warned me it's possible to get lost within ten minutes of going into the bush. You start wandering in circles.'

'As long as we keep climbing upwards we'll be all right.' Roger assured her.

'It's the coming down I'm worried about.'

'C'mon, we must hurry if we are going to have our picnic lunch on the summit – hey! What's that?'

There was a crack like the sound of a gun.

'Something's coming,' said Susan in a quiet voice. 'It must have stepped on a dead branch.'

They peered down the track and saw a shape appear out of a deep shadow. It was a boy wearing only khaki shorts and a beaming smile.

'Mani, what are you doing here?' cried Susan with relief.

'If you *pakehas* must climb the mountain I could not let you get lost in the bush,' he answered.

'But if you come with us you'll be breaking the *tapu*.'

'Who cares,' said Mani bravely. 'I reckon it's only a stupid old story after all.'

'But it works for Maoris – remember the story of the bulldozer driver . . .' began Roger.

'Shut up,' hissed Susan, and turning to Mani she said: 'Thanks, Mani. You can share our meal with us at the top.'

'You follow me, then,' said Mani, pleased he had now proved to the two English children that he was not afraid of the legend.

Roger and Susan toiled after the Maori boy, often stumbling over rotten logs which lay half buried in the soft mould produced by centuries of leaf fall.

'If the mountain is *tapu*, who made this track?' panted Roger.

'Deer,' answered Mani, and Susan thought Roger was tactless to keep mentioning that word. Half an hour later the trees began to thin out and looking up the three friends could see patches of blue sky. Soon afterwards the bush had changed into shoulder-high manuka scrub.

Roger wiped his perspiring face with his handkerchief and saw bloodstains on it.

'Your face is badly scratched,' Susan remarked. 'Of course, if you've spent your life in a London suburb, you can't be expected to be able to look after yourself in a forest'

He was about to make a retort about 'country bumpkins' – because she had lived in a Dorset village – but he bit back the words. The last thing he really wanted to do was to quarrel with this attractive girl.

10

Ahead of them Mani called: 'I'm out of the manuka now. It'll be easy after this.'

Susan forced herself through the last of the brittle bushes and found herself standing beside Mani on a stretch of yellow grass. The ground sloped upwards to the flat top of the mountain. It was dotted with outcrops of rock which thousands of years of wind and rain had sculpted into queer shapes.

'It won't be difficult to get to the top if we choose our way carefully,' Mani said.

Susan turned to make sure that Roger had not yet emerged from the manuka and then said quietly, 'Listen, Mani, you have got us here safely so there's no need for you to come further. We can have our picnic here, and if Roger has to get to the top, you and I can wait for him here.'

'I told you, Susan, I'm not scared now,' protested Mani. 'I was just kidding yesterday about that old Mist Lizard.' But Susan noticed that as he spoke his eyes were roaming the peak.

At that moment Roger blundered out of the scrub.

'We're having the picnic here,' announced Susan.

'Who says?'

'I do!'

'Oh.' He saw that she was determined so he gave her his knapsack with the food in it and, pulling off his shirt, stretched himself out to soak up the sunshine.

Half an hour later he drank the last of Mrs Ronson's home-made ginger beer and climbed lazily to his feet

'Time to push on.'

'Mani and I are staying here,' Susan said. 'You can play at being Sir Edmund Hillary by yourself.'

'I'm not staying,' cried Mani. 'I'm going up with Roger.'

'Oh – all right, I suppose I'll have to come too

11

then,' Susan said, and inwardly she added: 'And don't blame me if your wretched Mist Lizard thing gets you!'

They tackled the slope, hauling themselves up by grasping handfuls of grass or small stunted bushes. Now they were above the bush they had a panoramic view and in the distance could make out the tiny red roofs of the sheep station. Beyond it the river looked like a silver thread and further still an olive plain dotted with white specks of sheep rolled towards the heat haze in the east.

'What a wonderful sight,' gasped Roger. 'It makes the climb worth it.'

'It makes me feel dizzy,' said Susan. 'Come on, excelsior and all that!'

The ridge they were following ended at two pillars of reddish rock, beyond which a more gentle slope of flower-starred grass stretched up to the flat top of the mountain. As they approached the rocks Roger paused and pointed to where wisps of cloud seemed to be gathering above it.

'That's funny,' he said to himself as they passed between the natural gateway, 'a moment ago the sky was clear.'

They walked in silence up the alpine meadow and looking up again saw that more wraiths of clouds were forming. These swayed as though caught in a whirlwind, which seemed strange because it was such a hot calm day.

'There's something very odd about that cloud,' Susan cried. As she spoke it began to change colour and take on a new shape, to harden into something huge and solid – and alive.

Roger was hardly aware of Susan's cry of surprise or Mani's yell of pure terror. Instead he gazed with wide eyes at the gigantic creature which had grown out of the mist and was advancing towards him down the slope. It measured forty feet from its huge blunt head to the tip of its kangaroo-like tail; the body, being covered with a grey-green scaly hide. Its massive hind legs propelled it with a clumsy hopping motion, the "hands' of its forearms merely touching the ground from time to time to give it balance. Although these arms looked ridiculously small compared to the rear limbs, Roger realized they were large enough to seize him and lift him to its gaping sword-toothed jaws.

The children stood petrified as it drew nearer, its golden-eyed head swaying angrily while a low rumble echoed from its pulsating throat of yellowish skin. Suddenly it paused, reared to its full terrible height and screamed its hunting cry with gusts of breath so foul that Roger thought he would be sick. The sound was like that of a Jumbo jet at take-off, a sound that had all the fury of the death roar of the last dinosaur. Its long claws, filthy with mud and dried blood, slashed the air as it prepared to lunge at its victims.

The shriek of the monstrous lizard roused Roger from his trance. He turned to see Mani frozen with fear and Susan holding her arms out as though to protect herself. Roger gave the Maori boy a punch which sent him reeling back down the slope. Then, gripping Susan by the arm, he raced down the meadow and through the twin columns of rock. Moments later the three children were crashing through the manuka scrub in the direction of fhe comforting bush.

Branches tore their clothes and lashed their faces as they plunged on, always expecting to see the shadow of the nightmare reptile fall over them. In Roger's ears rang its scream of fury which only died away as they reached the shelter of the forest. Although they were sobbing for breath they did not pause here. Mani led the way to the deer track, Roger dragging a near-hysterical Susan behind him.

* * *

They sat on the creek bank in silence, their feet

dangling in the cool water. Susan was still red-faced and tousled from the race through the bush, Mani gave a shudder every now and then. Roger seemed to be the calmest as he wrapped his soiled handkerchief round a nasty cut in his arm. A few minutes earlier – because they had been frightened – they had quarrelled among themselves.

'I warned you not to go up there,' Mani had said with chattering teeth.

'Nobody said you had to come,' snapped Roger.

'It's all your fault,' Susan said. 'It wouldn't have happened if you hadn't been so stubborn. Like all chauvinistic males you had to have your own way. No wonder my Mum's all for women's liberation.'

'It doesn't seem to have done her a lot of good,' he retorted. 'I don't blame your father for keeping away.'

Before she realized quite what she was doing, Susan swung her arm and scored a hearty slap on Roger's face. The blow had the effect of silencing them. Each felt ashamed of blaming the others, Roger could have kicked himself for reminding Susan of her mother and father's problems, and she could have done the same for hitting him. It had been so undignified!

They sat in silence, reliving their experience and trying to understand what had really happened.

'We mustn't behave like silly kids,' Roger announced at last "We've got to think this thing out or it'll worry us for the rest of our lives.'

Susan nodded her agreement

'Now we all saw the Mist Lizard up there, but what was it that we actually saw?' he asked.

'If you don't know now you never will,' Mani said.

'Tell me what you saw then?'

'I saw this huge great lizard – just like a giant *tuatara* – that's what I saw.'

'What's a *tuatara*?'

'I know – we covered it in Biology at school,'

14

cried Susan. 'It's a New Zealand lizard, about a foot long, that survived from prehistoric times.'

This one wasn't a foot long,' declared Mani. 'It was as big as a truck.'

'And what did you see Sue?'

'The lizard of course. It was like a gigantic alligator. I saw it form out of the mist, and when it became solid it came slithering down the hillside, hissing like a hundred electric kettles.'

'And what I saw was a Tyrannosaurus Rex'

'A Tyrannosaurus what?' asked Susan.

'It was the most fearsome prehistoric reptile that ever lived,' explained Roger. 'It was a huge flesh-eating lizard. I've seen the skeleton of one at the Kensington Science Museum. But the important thing is – we each saw something different. What we saw must have been in our minds. Obviously for Mani a terrifying lizard would be a giant tuatara. You, Sue, must have seen alligators at the zoo, and I'll never forget seeing that Tyrannosaurus skeleton when I was younger. What happened was that we saw what we each imagined the Mist Lizard would be like. But it was a delusion.'

'Some delusion!' exclaimed Mani. 'Perhaps you are right, Roger, but it was breaking the *tapu* which made us see it'

'I don't think so,' said Roger. 'If *tapu* only works with Maoris, how was it that both Sue and I saw something?'

'I don't care how it happened, all I know is that I saw it because I broke the *tapu*.' Mani said. 'If you hadn't hit me that lizard would have got me. We only got away in the nick of time. Now I'm going home and I'm going to try and forget it Anyway, it's my turn to help with the milking. Best we tell no one about it or I'll be in trouble with my Dad for going up there.'

Susan and Roger agreed.

'Before you go, tell me what sort of noise did your lizard make,' Roger added.

'It growled,' said Mani.

'It hissed like I told you,' said Susan.

'Mine screamed,' Roger said thoughtfully. 'So our ears must have been deluded like our eyes.'

'I'm off,' said Mani. 'Don't forget it's a secret. See you tomorrow. Hooray!' He ran off along the bank.

'What did he mean – hooray?' asked Susan. 'Sounded like he was pleased to see the last of us.'

'I couldn't blame him if he was,' replied Roger. 'But in New Zealand it's a way of saying cheerio.'

'Let's go back to the sheep station,' Susan said. 'I just want to forget the last couple of hours, I'll never go near that mountain again. I can't believe it was a delusion as you say, I think it was something left over from the past which lives up there – like the Loch Ness Monster or the Abominable Snowman. Just because we described it differently doesn't mean a thing. What's so different about an alligator and a lizard . . .'

'But whatever it was that I saw stood up on two legs. An alligator couldn't have done that. Besides, if there really was something living up on the mountain top it would have been spotted before now.'

'And it probably was. That's why the Maoris believed the place was dangerous. And because there are often clouds round a mountain top it got the name of the Mist Lizard. Anyway, I'm going for a horse ride. Want to come?'

Roger nodded, but as he stood up to go he still looked very thoughtful.

* * *

Next morning the sun was just climbing over the rim of the eastern plains when Roger left the Ronsons' house with an airline bag slung from his shoulder. A

16

pencil line of smoke rose from the kitchen chimney where the cook was preparing the shepherds' breakfast, a reminder to the boy that he would miss his own meal. But he soon forgot his hunger as he took the track which would lead him again to the high lair of the monster.

3 The Greenstone Door

It was mid-morning when Roger broke through the belt of manuka scrub and, with pounding heart, gazed up at the twin rocks. The only sign of life was a black weka bird running through the grass in front of him. An ominous hush hung over the mountain and the brilliant blue of the sky was unmarked by cloud – no spirals of mist hung above the summit.

Nervously he unzipped his Air New Zealand bag and took out a digital camera which his uncle had left behind him at the Ronsons' home. He checked that it was ready for use, then advanced up the slope.

It took him longer than he remembered to reach the stone pillars which stood like a gateway to the unknown. Perhaps, as he had to admit to himself, he was slow because he was almost too terrified to pass through them. When he forced himself to do so he looked up and saw untidy strands of mist had appeared and were swirling together. As he watched they formed a dreadfully familiar shape.

Roger stood paralysed while the vapour-creature began to descend towards him, its colour changing as the mist appeared to become solid. As the day before the Tyrannosaurus Rex was propelled by the piston-like thrust of its rear legs while the claws at the end of its smaller forearms cut furrows in the sparse turf as it balanced itself. Again there was the terrible jet-like scream as the creature rose erect, the sun flashing on its golden eyes and yellowed fangs.

Roger aimed the camera and held his ground long enough to press the button. Then, as the greatest hunting creature the world had ever known was about to seize him with its talons, he turned and fled. Only when he was back in the bush and the cry of the monster was an echo in his ears did he stop and sink down with his back against the trunk of a red-berried rata tree.

When his hands had steadied, he saw that the camera screen showed the mountain scene exactly as it had been when he had taken it five minutes before except for one thing – there was no Mist Lizard!

'I was right,' Roger cried aloud. 'It only lives in my imagination. Now I can go to the very top.'

Again he approached the alpine meadow and again the mist formed at the summit, solidifying into the Cretaceous reptile. Roger gazed at it calmly, almost enjoying the sight of it as he would an adventure film.

'Come on, old monster, you're only inside my mind,' he shouted. 'Now I'll see what I can do with you. You might look prettier another colour.'

In his mind's eye Roger concentrated on imagining the creature a vivid shade of pink. As it halted and opened its wide jaws to emit a challenge, a change began to come over it The throat, normally an unpleasant slug-like hue, changed colour as though it was blushing. The rosy tint grew deeper and deeper until the throat was shocking pink, a colour which began to suffuse throughout the whole body. The scream of the Tyrannosaurus died as though the pilot of a jet plane had decided to shut down his motors, then the edges of the creature began to dissolve into pinkish smoke. When Roger stared up the meadow all that remained of the Mist Lizard was a patch of vapour.

Laughing aloud at his victory, the boy toiled up the slope to the flat, rock strewn summit. He was out of breath when he reached it and for some minutes he sat on a half-buried boulder to get it back, enjoying the view. To the east were the rolling plains, to the west the Awapuni Ranges. Then his mind went back to the riddle of the apparition.

What made us think we saw a monster, he mused. *There must be something strange up here to trigger-off such mental images. I must have a look around.*

He began walking among the rocks. Suddenly he came upon a saucer-shaped hollow which, in its centre, became a funnel disappearing below ground like a wide well shaft

I wonder if there's any greenstone here, thought Roger, approaching the depression. *It looks like an old volcano blow-hole.*

He carefully stepped to the edge of the shadowed opening and attempted to peer down it. As he did so his foot slipped on some loose pebbles, and leaning back to regain his balance he felt his other foot begin to slide. He waved his arms frantically as he fought to steady himself and then, almost before he realized what was happening, Roger had tumbled over the funnel edge and was sliding down it amid an avalanche of small stones.

He felt a shock of pain jolt up both legs, telling him that he had reached the end of his wild slide. As his eyes grew accustomed to the deep shadow he found he had not reached the bottom of the shaft, but had been caught on a narrow rock ledge. With a shudder he saw that if it had not halted him he would have continued down the hole which became almost vertical and the depth of which he could not even guess at.

Roger looked up to the blue circle above him and tried to discover a way back. The walls of the funnel were too steep and smooth to climb, so he began examining the ledge. Pressing hard against the rock, he edged along to where it appeared to end. But did it? Carefully getting down on his knees he looked over the side and saw another edge of rock about a foot below it, and another beyond that and another and then he realized that he had found a rough-hewn staircase spiralling down into the darkness of the shaft.

* * *

'Roger . . . Roger . . . where are you?'

The words echoed in the funnel, causing him to look up to the round patch of sky above him. He had been sitting despondently on the ledge, trying to work out a way to escape. So far all his efforts had ended with bleeding fingers and scraped knees. Now he climbed to his feet and shouted back: 'I'm here. Be careful of the edge, it's dangerous.'

The figure of Susan appeared silhouetted against the sky.

'Roger,' she called crossly, 'what on earth are you doing down there?'

'Never mind that now. The point is, how am I to get out?'

'I suppose I'll have to go and get help. You just can't be trusted alone. If it wasn't for the fact you'd left your airline bag up here I wouldn't have thought of looking down that hole. Perhaps if I bring a rope . . . whoops!'

As she spoke Susan swayed and began to slide down the slope just as Roger had done. He managed to catch her round the waist when she reached the ledge.

'That was near,' she gasped as he lowered her into a sitting position.

'You're not hurt?'

'I'll bet my legs and bottom are black and blue.'

'What brought you here Sue?'

'I was searching for you, silly. I thought you'd sneak back, and when I saw the camera had gone I was sure. I guessed you wanted to be the first to photograph the Mist Lizard. But when I came up the mountain it didn't appear. Has it gone?'

'It turned pink and blew away.' Seeing her bewildered expression in the dim light he added: 'I'll explain later. Now, look what I found.' And he pointed to the steps cut in the curving rock wall.

'I'll bet it's got something to do with the ancient people who carved the stele,' he continued excitedly. 'Perhaps it is a mine. I'd like to go down.'

'But would it be safe?'

'Should be, the steps are cut out of solid rock. But we really ought to be thinking of a way out'

Susan was looking at the steps with interest.

'Let's explore first. There may be greenstone down there and then we might make a lot of money. Luckily I've got my torch in my windcheater pocket, I was using it last night to go to the . . . you know.'

'Luckily for us the station loo is out of doors. At least we'll have some light, if the lamp wasn't broken in your slide.'

Susan took the flat torch from her pocket and switched it on. A beam of light illuminated the steps.

'Splendid.' cried Roger. 'I'll go first. Keep close to the wall.'

'I'll go first.' declared Susan, carefully putting her foot on the top step. 'Why should you go first just because you are a boy?'

'All right, all right. We won't argue.'

They worked their way down the curving steps and when Susan had counted forty they found themselves on the rock floor at the bottom of the shaft. She swept the beam about her and suddenly gave a cry as a human skull leered up at her. As she moved the torch its light revealed a skeleton sprawled at their feet

'Poor chap,' muttered Roger soberly, 'He wasn't as lucky as us. He must have missed the ledge when he slipped. It looks as though he's been there for years and years.'

'I suppose when he disappeared his family must have thought the Mist Lizard had got him.' said Susan. She swept the beam about the circular rock walls. 'They're so smooth they must have been cut with tools.'

'Hey, look,' cried Roger. 'Give me some light over here.' Susan obeyed and they saw a square tunnel mouth.

'It must be a greenstone mine.'

'My turn to go first,' said Roger firmly. He took the torch out of her hand and entered the six-foot-high passage. As he walked along the floor which gently sloped downwards he said to Susan who was close behind: 'You're right. This tunnel has been excavated with tools, you can see the marks. Uncle will be delighted.'

The corridor widened and split in two.

'Which?' asked Susan.

'Let's toss, tails the left fork,' Roger suggested. From her pocket Susan took out a New Zealand ten-cent piece and spun it in the air. When it tinkled on the floor the heads side was up and Roger strode into the right-hand passage. But as he put his foot down it met empty air where he expected to find solid floor.

He twisted wildly as he felt himself fall forward, and managed to grip the edge of the rock. His legs flayed as he struggled to heave his body to safety. Susan seized his shirt and added her strength so that he was able to squirm back on to the floor. After getting his breath back he picked up the torch and sent its light beyond the edge over which he had nearly plunged. The beam lost itself in utter darkness and the boy could not repress a shudder.

'Oh Roger, I think we'd better go back. This is dangerous.'

'First let's just look down the other tunnel. I've a hunch there's something very interesting down here. That pit was obviously a trap like the pits they had in old castles called oubliettes, so there must be something worth

23

guarding here. I'll look at the floor all the way from now on.' They took the left passage.

'We'd better not go too far,' Susan said after five minutes. 'I'm afraid the torch is starting to dim.'

'You're right . . . hold on, look at the ceiling.' Roger sent the beam along it.

'It has a pattern of large squares carved on it,' said Susan.

'Yes, now look at the floor.'

She saw that instead of smooth rock the floor was made of square slabs of stone.

'They must have been laid for some purpose,' mused Roger. 'The squares on the ceiling seem to relate to them. Some are sunken – now, why?'

'While you puzzle over ancient building techniques I'm going on,' declared Susan. 'I don't like it down here and I want to get it over.'

She placed her foot on one of the slabs, but immediately Roger grabbed her by the elbow and jerked her back. A second later a block of stone crashed from the ceiling, shattering into fragments on the slab where Susan should have been standing. For a moment she was speechless, then muttered: 'Thank you, Roger.'

'Only returning the compliment,' he replied with a shaky laugh. 'Look, the square above the slab you trod on was sunken. It was really the bottom of the block that fell. It's an ancient booby trap and I'll bet it's to safeguard some fabulous treasure. The Egyptians used to guard their tombs with obstacles and curses . . .'

'All we need is a curse!'

'But we have the key. If we walk on the flags beneath the squares which are not sunken we'll be all right'

'I think we ought to get Daddy.'

Roger was already testing his theory, putting his weight on a slab and leaping back. Nothing happened.

24

'Follow me exactly,' he said stepping carefully from slab to slab, following the pattern in the ceiling. A minute later the children found that the floor became solid rock again. The passage curved and led into a small square chamber, the far wall of which had a triangular arch containing a door of carved greenstone.

'It must be the entrance to a tomb,' cried Roger. 'The decoration on it is something like those in the photographs your Dad took of the stele. Whoever carved that must have built this place. Look at those inscribed spirals, and the hieroglyphs mixed up with them.'

It reminds me of Snakes and Ladders;' Susan said, and she began to trace her finger through the maze-like pattern. 'Look, I've made it to home.' Her finger came to the end of a groove in the centre of the triangular door.

There was a muffled sound of hidden mechanisms coming to life. The door rose slowly and from the opening streamed brilliant golden light which dazzled the children.

4 Sleeping Beauty

For a moment Roger thought that they had found an opening in the side of the mountain and it was daylight flooding over them. As his eyes adjusted he saw that the passage continued beyond the triangular archway.

'How can light have lasted so long?' Susan asked. 'It must have been burning for centuries. It's impossible.'

Roger nodded. Underground doors which opened themselves and light without visible source was beyond him. Yet he was filled with an excitement he had never felt before. This was how Howard Carter must have felt when he opened a sealed door and beheld the treasures of Tutankhamun. He took Susan by the hand and led her through the arch.

Beyond it they found the passage was triangular too, and after about twenty feet it ended in a door identical to the one Susan had so unexpectedly opened. While Roger examined this Susan looked at the walls which, instead of being roughly hewn, were smooth like black glass.

Suddenly the silence was broken by a grinding sound which made her heart race.

'Roger, the door!'

As she spoke she raced back along the passage, but she was too late. The greenstone door was back in position. Seen from this side it was perfectly smooth without any carving for her fingers to trace.

'We're trapped,' she gasped. Suddenly she felt as though her strength had drained from her and she sank on the floor, leaning her back against the angled wall. Roger sat beside her.

'Like rats in a trap!' he muttered bitterly. 'But there's got to be some reason. Everything works too efficiently for it to be some ancient tomb. No one had a lighting system like this a century ago, let alone thousands of years.'

'Who would run a place like this – secret agents?' Susan asked. 'Or could it be some hush-hush rocket site hidden inside the mountain?'

'Perhaps it's a base built by space beings who came in flying saucers; there've been a lot of UFO sightings in New Zealand.' For a moment the idea cheered him up.

'But whatever it is – are we going to starve to death here?'

Roger shook his head. To reassure Susan he said he thought something would happen soon. And he was right

'Everything seems to be going hazy,' Susan cried. 'What is it, Roger?'

'Seems like some kind of smoke, but where can it be coming from?'

They looked round wildly, suddenly afraid of being gassed, but there were no vents in the gleaming black walls. The whitish cloud just materialized out of the air and floated in layers about them. Susan held her breath until her face went red with the effort, then her agonized lungs forced her to take a deep shuddering breath.

The vapour seemed to have no effect on her. She did not choke or sneeze, but soon she wondered if it was making her light-headed. She fancied she could hear music, but it was not like any music she had heard before and she could not recognize the instruments producing it.

The strange sounds made her feel as though she was floating upwards, rising like a bubble through a tropical sea, up and up until it seemed that at any moment

27

she would break through its surface into glorious sunshine. She forgot her fear and turned to Roger to see that he was smiling.

'Can you hear it?'

'Yes, it's marvellous, but where is it coming from?' She pointed beyond him to where the second door was rising just as the first had done, and through the aperture the majestic sound swelled. Roger climbed to his feet. The unearthly music made him feel that he had accomplished something wonderful. It was as though by braving the Mist Lizard and getting past the dangers in the tunnel he was being welcomed by the soaring harmonies.

He helped Susan up and hand in hand the they walked through the triangular arch into a fantastic new world.

* * *

At first Roger could not make out where he was. Then, by the same mysterious radiance which had illuminated the passage he could see that they were in a vast three-sided hall, the walls of which sloped gradually inwards until they met at their apex.

'It must be a space alien's base,' he said in a hushed voice. 'Look at those – those things under those huge glass domes.'

'No, it's a tomb from a lost civilization. The ancient Egyptians buried chariots and things with their mummies, and some forgotten race must have done the same here. And do you realize what this whole place is?'

'It certainly reminds me of something,' he answered, his eyes running over the rows of huge transparent bubbles protecting objects whose use he could not even guess at,

'It's a pyramid, we're inside a hollow pyramid,' Susan exclaimed. 'I'll bet it was built on top of the mountain and got covered by a volcanic eruption.'

Roger walked over the to one of the domes which held a tall shape made up of crystal cubes, glowing with all the colours of the rainbow. It made him think of something a young child might have constructed out of a giant set of Lego.

'It's unbelievable,' he murmured. 'Not only is the air pure but there's no dust. No ancient tomb could be like this.'

'Look here,' cried Susan in a delighted voice. She was gazing into the next dome in which stood a large glass sphere on a black pedestal. In its centre three-dimensional patterns appeared and disappeared at regular intervals, each made up of lines of coloured light.

'It's like a telly that's gone funny,' she said. 'Only it's rather beautiful. I'll bet this was some sort of museum where they put their most prized inventions,'

'Who's *they*?'

'The Atlanteans. I'll bet this goes back to the Lost Continent of Atlantis.'

Together they wandered among the domes, each containing some puzzling object. After a few minutes they found themselves at an open space in the centre of the triangular hall.

'Look,' gasped Susan. 'It can't be true.'

'It's the tomb this place was built for.'

'But she can't be dead . . .'

'She couldn't have lived since Atlantis or whenever it was they put her in that glass coffin.'

They were gazing at a long case of diamond-hard crystalline material which stood on an oblong slab of marble. Inside lay the body of a beautiful young woman clad in a gown woven of golden thread. Her long, almost white hair was carefully arranged over her shoulders and her hands were peacefully clasped under her breasts. A ring sparkled on her finger which seemed to generate its own light. There was a slight smile on her lips and it was easy to imagine that she had only closed her eyes a few minutes earlier.

'The Sleeping Beauty,' murmured Susan.

'A prince couldn't wake her,' said Roger, 'there's no lid to the coffin.'

'There's some strange lettering carved below it I'll bet it says she was a princess.'

For a while they stood in awed silence, then Roger said, 'It's uncanny, that music is still playing. No ancient people could record music, let alone have it playing centuries later. I think she's from another planet, she looks almost too beautiful to be human . . .'

'Oh dear, what can we do?' cried Susan with a note of dismay in her voice.

'What do you mean?'

'If we tell people about this place it'll be in the newspapers and on telly, and everything will be disturbed and the poor princess will be put on show in some museum.'

'We'll only tell your father,' said Roger. 'He'll know what to do. But we have to get out of here first.'

Reluctantly they turned and walked back to the door and into the passage. The music faded and the greenstone door closed behind them.

* * *

Professor Simon White sat cross-legged outside his tent while a Primus stove hissed beneath a pan of soup. The dying sun cast a long shadow from the carved stone pillar which held the gaze of the English archaeologist. His thoughts were abruptly interrupted by the roar of an engine overhead, and he looked up to see the yellow helicopter descend into the clearing. As its rotor blade hissed to a stop Scott Baker opened the door and called out cheerfully: 'Got a surprise for you, Prof. She bullied me into it . . .'

30

And there was Susan, climbing out of the machine with a pack and a rolled-up sleeping bag.

'Hello, Daddy. Thought I'd come and keep you company. Hope you're glad to see me.'

'Er – of course. It's just that I didn't expect you. What about Roger?'

'Oh, he's all right . . .'

Father and daughter waved as the helicopter rose into the flame-coloured sky.

'Now, my girl, what's all this about?' the Professor asked, as the clatter of the aircraft became muffled by the surrounding bush. 'Is there something wrong?'

'Oh, no, Daddy. I've got something dreadfully important to tell you. You must promise to let me tell it right through and not laugh at me. It's deadly serious.'

'Promise,' he said. 'Fire away.'

With her eyes fixed on the bubbling soup Susan told her father of the adventure right up to the time they found the girl in the transparent tomb.

'It's utterly fantastic,' muttered the Professor when she ran out of words. 'It's so fantastic I'm not sure you aren't making it all up. It's not April first is it?'

She shook her head.

'I wouldn't lie to you. Daddy.'

'Hmmm. I just don't know what to say. You and Roger may have stumbled on the greatest archaeological find of all time. But I don't understand about that mist dragon or whatever it was.'

'Neither do we.'

'How did you get out when you left the tomb?'

'This time the second door just seemed to open by itself and we went back to the shaft. We climbed up the steps to the ledge and we found some handholds cut in the rock. They were above our heads and we would never have discovered them without the torch. Roger lifted me up to them, and then I was able to give him a hand.' She gave a little shudder: 'That was the worst part of the whole adventure. Poor Roger hates heights and he was as white as a ghost when we reached the top.'

'So now?'

'So now, Daddy, we want you to come and see it for yourself, and we don't want anyone else to know. I've brought a large-scale map so we can find our way through the bush to the mountain where we'll meet Roger. I told the Ronsons I wanted to stay with you for several days, and Roger will make up some story about camping out so we'll have enough time without people worrying about us.'

'I've got a crafty daughter,' the Professor laughed. 'All right, we'll set off at the crack of dawn. But I can't help feeling you dreamed it all.'

* * *

It was mid-afternoon when Simon White and Susan toiled to the top of the mountain where they found Roger seated on a rock.

'Hello,' panted the Professor. 'Do you go along with this extraordinary story my daughter has been telling me?'

'Absolutely, and we'll prove it to you,' the boy answered. 'It'll be much easier this time because I've brought a strong rope and a powerful torch with plenty of batteries.'

He led them over to the funnel. They climbed down and soon were walking along the underground passage. This time the traps held no fear for them. When they reached the greenstone door Roger held the torch while Susan began to trace the complicated pattern with her finger.

'It seems to me that it's a sort of basic intelligence test,' said the Professor. 'Whoever constructed the mausoleum didn't want savages to get in. Hmm, very interesting,' he added as the door rose as before and the unearthly music echoed about them. 'But no tomb builders would want the tomb to be entered. Such places never had entrances, the original opening was always sealed. Are you certain this is a tomb?'

'You'll see,' said Susan. Again the white gas flowed round them and then the second door opened.

'It just can't be,' exclaimed the Professor, his voice high-pitched with excitement as he gazed at the domes and their strange contents.

'What can't be, uncle?' asked Roger.

'I'm starting to think what this place might be,' he answered. 'Where's the sarcophagus?'

They led him to where the girl lay in her coffin, the same light smile on her lips which they had seen the day before. After a minute he dropped to his knees and began examining the carving on the base of the tomb.

'Susan believes that New Zealand must have been part of Atlantis once,' said Roger, 'but I think it's something to do with flying saucers. Perhaps that girl was a member of the crew of one which landed here ages ago. When she died her friends must have built this tomb for her in their base. Somehow they arranged the Mist Lizard to frighten intruders away.'

The Professor did not answer him. He was absorbed with the designs.

'Is it some sort of ancient writing – hieroglyphs or pictographs?' Susan asked nearly half an hour later during which she had got rather bored with her father's silent concentration.

'They're pictographs all right,' he said straightening up painfully. 'Look closely and you can see it's almost like a stylized comic strip. This panel shows the pyramid being built, and the next the girl being brought into it. Here she is laying herself down before the coffin was placed over her . . .'

33

'You mean she was alive?' cried Susan in horror.

'She certainly was.'

'But that's only in the first three panels,' said Roger. 'There are plenty more. What do they tell us?'

'You're perfectly right,' said the Professor. 'They contain pictorial instructions on how to revive her. That girl – unless I am utterly mistaken – is in a state of suspended animation.'

'You don't mean . . .' gasped Susan and Roger together.

'Yes, incredible as it may seem, she could still be alive.'

5 Neerak Awakes

Susan and Roger sat on their sleeping bags watching the Professor who was kneeling in front of the pictographs, jotting notes in his pocket book. He had been concentrating on them for several hours and once, when Susan had suggested he might stop for some cocoa from the Thermos flask, he was angry at being interrupted.

'I can't believe that girl is still alive,' said Susan. 'She must have been lying there for ages and ages.'

'It's hard to believe that anything here is real,' Roger replied. 'What machinery, capable of lifting doors, supplying light and playing music, would have lasted so long in working condition? Ah, it looks as though uncle has finished at last.'

The burly archaeologist straightened up painfully and came over to the children.

'I've done the best I could,' he announced wearily. 'The pictorial parts were quite straightforward, but I'm not so sure about those symbols. I only hope I have understood them correctly, that girl's life could depend upon it . . .'

'You're going to wake her?' cried his daughter, her eyes bright with excitement.'

'Yes. I've thought it over and I think it's best that we should do it rather than inform the world and have a circus act made out of it. You can imagine what it would be like with hordes of newspapermen and newsreel cameras, politicians and so-called experts. That sort of thing is all right for an astronauts' splash-down, but not for someone who's been in a trance for perhaps thousands of years. Imagine the shock.'

'How are you going to do it?' Roger asked.

'By following the instructions of the pictographs step by step. I've written it down like a script – probably it's just a question of activating automatic processes. The geniuses who designed this place must have worked out her re-entry into life very thoroughly.'

'Then what do you believe this place to be?' asked Susan.

'What's known as a "time capsule". When Cleopatra's Needle was erected on the Thames Embankment in 1878 coins, newspapers and everyday objects were sealed in a space under the monument so that in the far distant future people could gain some picture of Victorian life. The idea spread and it became quite a common practice in the foundations of new buildings. I think this pyramid was the same sort of thing but on a magnificent scale. There must have been a bygone race of people who reached a standard of civilization far in advance of ours; and they left behind them this Time Pyramid with examples of their culture in it.'

'But why haven't we some knowledge of them? We learn all about the ancient Egyptians at school, and the Babylonians.'

'Perhaps there are clues but we have not been able to recognize them. It's an interesting point that the pyramid is the most enduring structure from ancient times. Some memory of pyramid building may have remained after the people who built this one vanished to inspire the Egyptian engineers.'

'But why should such a clever race not survive?' Roger wanted to know.

'Perhaps they were destroyed by a natural calamity, perhaps by a plague. If we can revive the girl we may find out the answers. They must have guessed that after their civilization Man would become primitive again, as in Dark Age England after Roman civilization fell. So they safeguarded this place by traps and puzzles to make sure that only people who had reached a certain standard could awaken the sleeper. It takes a degree of knowledge to translate those designs, and it's lucky I've spent my life studying such things.'

Followed by the children the Professor returned to the marble slab on which the smiling girl lay. At one end, outside the glass-like case, there was a pattern of glowing jewels set in the stone.

'These are not for decoration, they are really control buttons,' he explained. 'Even these were designed to prevent the sleeper falling into the wrong hands. If barbarians had managed to break in they would have wrenched them out for loot and the girl could never have been revived. According to the pictographs, I have to press them in a certain sequence. If it is done in the wrong order it might be fatal. The emerald first.'

Gently he laid the tip of his forefinger on a square stone which flashed green fire.

'Now the ruby – and we wait for something to start happening.'

Peering into the case Susan and. Roger saw that it was filling with an opaque vapour which reminded them of the gas in the passage. The details of the sleeper became hazy as it covered her. A minute later it began to ebb away, and the Professor touched another of the jewels. This time a pale violet gas flowed over the still figure.

Susan gave a cry of excitement.

'She's alive. Look, she's starting to breathe.'

The sleeper's chest rose and fell as though she had taken a deep breath.

'It must be that gas which revives the heart and lungs,' muttered Professor White as he hastily touched a stone which sparkled like a diamond. The gas took on a deeper hue, and the girl's breathing became regular. Another jewel was pressed and the case began to lose its mauve tint as the vapour thinned and vanished.

'One more to go,' the Professor said, and Roger noticed that trickles of sweat were running down his face. 'Pray God I have not mistaken the instructions. There are two buttons left, and as a final precaution the wrong one could cause the sleeper to die. It must be this topaz.'

His finger stabbed the yellow gem and he looked up, almost afraid to see the effect. The children held their breath. Then, as they watched, the transparent material of the case dissolved into nothingness.

For nearly a minute the beautiful silver-haired girl lay breathing gently. Then she sighed and her eyelids fluttered open, and she yawned as though waking from a night's sleep. She raised her hand and ran her fingertips over her face, then took a strand of her hair and looked at it intently.

Suddenly an expression of fear flitted across her features and turning her head her sea-green eyes focused on the three figures who were gazing at her in wonder.

Slowly she sat up and, placing her hand on her heart, said in a low voice, 'Neerak.'

The Professor bowed and replied: 'Simon White.' Then he laid his hand on his daughter's shoulder and added: 'Susan.'

'Soo zaan,' the girl repeated and smiled. She held out her hand and Susan took it gently.

'Welcome to the twenty first century, Neerak,' she said.

* * *

'What's the matter with you, Roger?' Mani demanded. Roger was sitting on a fallen log by the swimming hole close to the Ronson sheep station.

'Nothing,' he answered moodily.

'He's often like that,' called Susan from the water where she was practising what she liked to believe was a fast crawl. 'He makes you gloomy just to look at him.'

'Now don't you start quarrelling again,' cried Mani. 'The last few days anyone would think you were enemies.'

It was true. For a week the children had been back at the sheep station, both trying to appear normal while their secret burned within them and as a result they took it out on each other. But when they were alone together their conversations would begin with such remarks as, 'I wonder how many English words Neerak has learned yet'

Professor White had told them they must stay at the station as though nothing had happened to avoid any suspicion, but he promised that as soon as he could communicate with the girl from the past they could return to the underground pyramid. He would explain to the Ronsons that he was taking the children to help him with a dig so that they would feel no anxiety about them.

Tonight, Roger was thinking, *Uncle is due back from the stele by helicopter to get stores. I wonder what news he'll have . . .* Then he turned his attention to hitting the surface of the water with a stick so it splashed in Susan's face and spoilt her stroke.

'Pig,' she spluttered at him. 'Rotten rotten pig.' After that Roger cheered up.

That evening the helicopter appeared like a giant yellow insect over the lawn and everyone crowded round as the Professor climbed out.

'Find any treasure, Prof?' called one of the shepherds.

Susan's father just smiled.

'It's going well, but this time I'll take Susan and Roger to help me with the work,' he said. The children felt like jumping for joy. His words meant that they would actually be able to speak to Neerak.

39

'Have you figured what that old carving is?' asked Gully as they walked to the verandah. 'I guess if it's real ancient I might get my picture in the paper again . . .'

'It's much older than I thought at first.' the Professor answered.

Just before the evening meal Susan managed to be alone with her father for a minute.

'How is Neerak?' she said breathlessly. 'Is she well? Can she understand you yet?'

'She's amazing,' he replied. 'Already she's speaking simple sentences. Mentally her race must have been much superior to us.'

'Do you know the history of the pyramid yet?'

'A little of it, but – I'll let her tell you herself. I found there is another level below the great hall where Neerak has her rooms and there are more machines. Do you know, there's even a flying machine in the Time Pyramid. It's round like a huge ball but goodness knows what makes it fly. I wish I was more scientific . . . And I believe there are other pyramids like this in different parts of the world. Ah, supper . . .'

'I wish I could tell Mani about it,' Susan said. 'I'd like to explain that the Mist Lizard is not real. I think he's still worried because he broke the *tapu*.'

'I know, but the time's not right yet. Neerak must be allowed to adjust before she comes into our world. And while there are many things in the pyramid which could help our civilization, there could be dangers . . . devices that in the wrong hands could be turned into weapons, like atomic power in our own time. We must be certain of what we're doing before we make any announcements. Now come on, Susie, I'm starving.'

She nodded. She was fairly good at keeping secrets but this was almost too much.

The next morning the helicopter made a couple of trips to the stele, first taking the professor and his supplies

40

and then Susan and Roger.

'Good luck,' called Scott Baker when they had disembarked in the clearing. 'See you next week.'

A minute later the noise of the machine faded and was replaced by the tiny rustling sounds caused by a warm wind flowing over the bush. The three adjusted their packs and began the trek to the *tapu* mountain and the Time Pyramid.

6 Secret History

As they trudged between the dark evergreen trees Roger kept asking his uncle all sorts of questions – what did Neerak eat? How many years had she slept? What were the strange objects under the glass domes? But Professor White merely shook his head and said the children would get the answers from Neerak herself. Once he paused to tighten the straps of his heavy pack.

'It's full of all the books and magazines I could get my hands on,' he explained. 'They'll give Neerak some idea of our world. She's very anxious to know what the women of the present day are wearing. You'll have to have some long chats with her, Susan.'

They were weary when they reached the summit of the mountain and descended into the passage which sloped down to the pyramid entrance. They noticed that when they approached the greenstone door it now opened of its own accord.

'The sensors have been adjusted to my vibrations,' the Professor said, but he did not have time to explain further as the second door slid upwards and the children raced into the three-sided hall. For the last week it had seemed as though they had dreamed the whole adventure, but here was the proof that it was real.

As they walked along a row of domes they saw Neerak coming towards them in a long gown of shimmering turquoise. Susan noticed that she had plaited her hair into a silver rope which she wore hanging down one side of her face.

42

'Hello,' she said with a slow smile. 'Welcome to the Time Pyramid, Soozan and Roger.'

'You speak English beautifully,' Susan burst out, 'How is it possible?'

'I had training in language learning before I became a Sleeper,' she answered, choosing her words carefully. 'Simon has worked very hard teaching me, and there are machines here which helped me. But come to my apartment where we can talk.'

She led them on to a large golden-coloured square set in the blue-black floor at one corner of the pyramid. When she dapped her hands the square sank gently to the room below. Its walls were made of some translucent material in which swirls of pure colour writhed in strange patterns,, sometimes blending together and then bursting into new shapes. Neerak showed the children how to sink into large spongy cubes which moulded comfortably to the contours of the sitter before becoming firm like ordinary chairs.

'Your father told me you would be full of questions, but first let me offer you a drink,' Neerak said. 'You all look very tired and thirsty.' She vanished through a triangular doorway. . .

'Gosh, what a place,' whispered Roger. 'Just look at that animated wallpaper . . . and furniture that almost thinks for itself.'

Neerak returned with a tray on which were simple glasses of blue liquid.

'In my time this drink was considered very refreshing after long journeys,' she said, handing round the glasses. Cautiously Roger sipped his, then his face broke into a smile.

'It's like cola, only much better,' he declared.

'Mine is like strawberry milkshake,' Susan said.

Roger looked at Neerak and asked, 'These are all the same really, aren't they?'

She nodded.

'But they taste different to each one of us. We are tasting what we want to taste. It's like the Mist Lizard – all in our minds.'

'You are right,' smiled Neerak. 'As the Mist Lizard was created out of your imaginations, likewise, the drink takes on the flavour you want it to. What are you drinking, Simon?'

'Lager and lime,' answered the professor.

'Then the whole pyramid could be something existing only in our minds,' persisted Roger. 'It may not be real at all.'

'It is real enough and now I shall tell you something of its history,' said Neerak.

'But first let me ask what you are drinking?' interrupted the professor.

'It was my favourite drink, the juice of the shiral fruit,' she laughed. 'there was a shiral tree growing at my home in Thool before the Sickness came.'

The children settled back comfortably to listen to history they knew they would never learn at school.

'Ages of time separate the world I knew from your world of today,' Neerak began. 'in the early days of my world there were many races on the earth with very simple civilizations. Then one group began to progress faster than the others. They were my ancestors who later came to be called Atlaans. Within a few centuries they changed from barbarians to law-abiding men who had explored the world, discovered medicine and sources of energy which gave each citizen the power of a hundred slaves at his command – with the result that human slavery was abolished. In less than one century they progressed from transport based on tame animals to flying machines which could not only circle the world but even voyage to the Moon . . .'

'So we were not the first,' breathed Roger.

'But my ancestors had to pay a price for their progress,' continued Neerak 'They learned to control the resources of the earth but they could not control themselves. While they were unlocking the secrets of the universe they also fought terrible wars among themselves. In each war more deadly weapons were developed until they had ones so terrible they knew that if they were used it would mean the end of themselves as well as their enemies. Yet they went on making them . . . such was their madness. Then something happened which changed everything.'

'They had an atomic war,' said Roger.

'No, they ran out of energy. To feed their great machines they bored deep into the earth to steal its wealth, and they used it as though it would last forever. Even when they realized supplies of oil and minerals were running low they did nothing to conserve them. Our history books called it The Age of Waste.

'They plundered the planet and within a score of years their wells ran dry and their mines were exhausted. Having depended on fossilized power sources they saw themselves doomed.

'But it turned out to be the saving of the race for without energy they were unable to go to war against each other. The flying machines rusted, and the great highways on which wheeled machines had once raced were used by animals pulling carts. As the years passed their tall towers tumbled down, for without power they could not repair or replace them, and their ports were graveyards for useless ships.

'Once again Man began to build vessels of wood which were propelled by the wind. Most people lived in the remains of their crumbling cities, slowly sinking back to an earlier way of life. They sowed their grains by hand in what had once been beautiful parks, and they hunted wild animals in the tunnels through which their linked cars had once thundered.

'They began to forget their history as the material for making records ran out. Parents did not bother to teach their children to decipher the old lettering – it was more important that they were skilled in the use of handlooms and crossbows. It seemed to be the sunset of Man – soon he would return to what he had been originally, a naked hunter.

'Then we got a second chance. A new power was found, a power undreamed of by the earlier scientists who had concentrated on chemical energy.'

Neerak paused and the Professor continued: They called it Cosmic Energy. It may have had something to do with magnetism, but it seems to be like nothing we know today. That is why the strange machines you see under the domes do not need to have moving parts. The important thing was that it was unlimited and there was no need to spoil the earth to harness it'

'But how was it discovered if the people had lost their knowledge and scientific skill?' Roger asked.

'It came to us from the stars,' said Neerak. 'A space vessel landed, from what corner of the universe it had begun its voyage we never knew. When it was opened it was found that the crew had died centuries before and become mounds of dust which told nothing of what sort of creatures they had been. The ship's driving force was still intact, and luckily there was an Atlaan genius able to analyse it. With the new knowledge Cosmic Energy generators were built and the Atlaan civilization flourished. But now Man had finally learned the lesson and he saw the utter stupidity of war.

'The new peaceful era, based on Cosmic Energy, was miraculous compared with the earlier one based on chemical power. With material gained from the inexhaustible energy source wonderful buildings and machines were made without the need to take minerals

46

from the earth. In the past energy had been created by the destruction or combustion of material – Cosmic Energy could be transformed into a material we called Plaax.

'It had many qualities which were unknown before, it could renew itself automatically so that objects made from it could never wear out (this pyramid is made from it), it could alter its shape at our wish and it could create energy within its cells so it was ideal for machines.

'The Atlaans lived longer and longer as their Masters of Medicine discovered the secrets of life itself, and it was not unusual for people to live for several hundred years. From Earth our Plaax spacecraft flew out to the galaxy driven almost at the speed of light by Cosmic Energy. Then, when it seemed we had gained everything that Man had sought after – knowledge, disease-free life and comfort – the new evil began.'

'How do you mean?' Susan asked in a puzzled voice.

'My people forgot they were still human. They were so powerful they became too proud even to look after themselves. They had a race of slaves to work and even think for them . . .'

'Slaves?'

'Yes, we created them,' Neerak continued. 'What was the word you used to describe them, Simon?'

'Robots,' said the Professor.

'Yes, robots. At first they were clumsy affairs, but how useful they were. It meant that Atlaans were able to live on a beautiful island continent in the most favoured part of the world while the robots harvested the ocean beds and worked the factories in the desert lands and on the polar ice.

'Then came the desire to make the slaves as much like ourselves as possible. It was a challenge to our scientists and they began to design robots which looked like humans, walked like humans and could control

47

themselves by devices set in their heads.'

'What we would call computers,' the Professor explained.

They were improved until we could give them their orders by speaking to them,' Neerak continued, 'And they could reply. In the robot laboratories they made others like themselves and each new model was superior to the last. Soon they were organizing everything for us, and we devoted ourselves to pleasure and the final puzzle . . .'

'The final puzzle?' repeated Roger.

'Time travel. Now that everything was efficiently controlled by the robots the Atlaan scientists were free to work on their dream of finding a way of visiting the past or future. They planned to go back through the ages almost as our starships went through space, and in this they were greatly helped by the calculating ability of specially designed robots. They had their first success before disaster overtook the Atlaans again.'

'What happened?' Susan asked.

'The robots began to think for themselves.'

For a moment Neerak sat lost in thought and then continued. 'It is hard to explain – the Atlaans never really understood it themselves. As the robots' thinking systems became more complex, so they were able to design even more complex ones, and so the process continued. At first this delighted their human masters. It amused them to have beautiful servants who could play games or talk intelligently with them, but who were still only mechanical slaves. But the progress of the robots was overshadowed by the interest in time travel.

'The first success came when our scientists had managed to send a small animal – a dog, do you call it? – a year back in time. They knew it must have worked because immediately after the experiment they found its bones – which were a year old.

'The question was could we alter history by going

back into the past? If we could send information back to people in the remote past the human race would have progressed much faster, and that would have an effect on the present The world would be suddenly different, and it would be possible that the Atlaans might no longer exist, even though they had caused the change by tampering with time . . .'

'It's mind-boggling,' declared Roger.

'Like trying to imagine the universe with no beginning and no end,' added Susan, 'I cannot think of it going on for ever, yet if it has a limit there must be something beyond that.'

'I know what you mean,' said Neerak, 'and the Atlaans never managed to discover the answers about time travel. The robots reached the stage where they could reason for themselves and they decided to destroy the human species and take over the earth.

'One morning, acting on a secret signal, they began to assassinate their masters. Suddenly these perfect servants turned on them in the streets and in their homes. And without their work the Atlaan civilization could not continue. But the rebels did not have a quick victory. Once it was realized what was happening the energy transmitters, which supplied power to the robots, were shut down and most of the slaves became frozen statues.

'This halted the rebellion on the island continent, but of course it did not affect the vast armies of robots which were employed in different parts of the world. They had their own power supplies and they began to prepare for war against the humans.

'The Atlaan Council decided the only chance of defeating the robot armies was to do something which had been unthinkable for generations – to use the terrible missiles which had remained in their towers from the days when men prepared for war against each other. One after another they streaked into the sky to destroy the robot colonies with – their – I am sorry I don't know the words.'

'Atomic warheads is what we'd call them,' supplied the Professor.

'The missiles were effective. The rebel centres were burned and the rays given off by the explosions damaged the delicate mechanisms of the robots who were outside the fire zones. But though the humans won, the cost was their own destruction. Poisonous clouds drifted across the face of the earth causing death and sickness to the Atlaans. They were unable to bear children, their blood thinned in their veins, and they realized that their race was doomed. As they prepared to meet the end with dignity they wondered whether it was possible for some form of intelligent life to survive in remote pockets – such as the very primitive humans who still dwelt in jungles.

'The Atlaans decided that their dying task would be to preserve their achievements for the benefit of future humanity should it survive and start developing again. They built ten of these pyramids in different parts of the world.'

'You mean there are nine others?' said Roger.

'Certainly they were built,' replied Neerak. 'Soon we will find out if they have survived, for it is my first duty to awaken any other Sleepers. The Atlaans' great fear over the Time Pyramids was that they would be entered by savages who would misuse the machines, so safeguards were designed. As you have found yourselves the pyramid has a device which affects the minds of those who come near, making them believe they see something so fearful that if they were primitive they would not dare venture near again.'

'So that explains the Mist Lizard,' said Susan.

'From what I can gather it was a form of hypnosis caused by waves from an automatic transmitter within the pyramid,' added her father. 'They put the suggestion of a monster in the mind of the trespasser, but allowed him or her to supply the details from their own imaginations. It would be more frightening that way as people would see what they feared most.'

'There were other safeguards, too,' continued Neerak, 'such as the intelligence test built into the pattern of the door . . .'

Susan smirked at Roger.

'What about the gas in the passage?' he asked.

'That was to kill harmful . . . what is the word, Simon?'

'Germs.'

'My people did not know what sort of world I might wake in so every precaution was taken to protect me. Over the ages new diseases might have developed against which I would have no resistance, so the gas was to purify those who entered until the Sleeper was able to make tests. I have found that your atmosphere is quite safe for me.

'Now that I have met you and Simon I believe that I have come into a good world, one that could put the contents of this pyramid to good use . . .'

Susan felt uncomfortable and wondered if her father had told Neerak about the other side of the present day world with war and hunger and people often not allowed to lead the lives they wished.

'If the Atlaans were poisoned by the radiation, how was it that you and the other Sleepers were expected to survive?' Roger asked.

'We were chosen from the few who accidentally escaped the radiation effects. I was staying with my mother and father in a holiday dome beneath the sea when the war began; some of the Sleepers were on the Moon at the time. We were sealed in special apartments, living in pure air which had been stored for the use in space vessels, and undergoing special mental training to enable us to learn languages quickly. It would be essential that

51

we could talk with whoever awakened us as soon as possible.

'I was chosen for the first Time Pyramid to be completed. My family and friends brought me here, and the Masters of Medicine prepared me for my trance while I said goodbye to them. It was very sad because I knew I would never see them again and that they only had a short time to live because of the Sickness. I remember lying down and taking the draught . . . and then nothing until I opened my eyes and saw you.'

Neerak fell silent. For a while nobody spoke, and then Roger was embarrassed to see a tear trickle down the girl's cheek as her mind filled with memories of her own time. Susan went over to her and put her arm round her shoulders, but she could think of nothing to say to comfort her.

'I am being weak,' said Neerak suddenly. 'I should not be thinking of myself, but my fellow Sleepers. Let us see if they have survived.'

7 Under the Ice

Neerak led them from her apartments to a small chamber bathed in pale blue light. In its centre, appearing to float a yard above the floor, was a large transparent ball.

'This will tell me of my companions' fate,' she said, touching a control panel set in the wall. The ball glowed with patches of green and blue light

'It's the world,' Susan gasped.

'It is,' agreed Neerak. 'The world as it is seen by tiny "eyes" which spin at a great height around the earth. They pick up a signal from each Time Pyramid which still exists.'

'They're what we would call satellites,' the Professor explained. The colours within the ball became firmer and Roger had the feeling that he was out in space looking at the earth as though he was an astronaut.'

'How it has changed,' Neerak remarked with a catch in her voice. 'The island continent which was my home is no more. All I can recognize are the ice-covered poles. How long have I been in a trance for the world to change so much?'

For a moment she was silent, a lonely figure gazing at the model of a planet which she felt was no longer hers. Then she turned to the controls again. Suddenly a pinhead of crimson light glowed close to the bottom of the floating sphere.

'Only one besides myself,' breathed Neerak. 'And it must be hidden in the icy wastes of the South Pole. We must go and awaken the Sleeper there.'

'Just a minute,' said, the Professor. 'We can't go just like that. A proper expedition needs to be organized.'

A determined look shone in Neerak's green eyes.

'People must not know of the Time Pyramids until the other Sleeper is brought back to life,' she declared. 'And you must come. It is not that I do not trust you, but I cannot leave you behind in case you reveal the secret by accident.'

'But how will we travel to Antarctica?'

'In the pyramid there is an Aerial Globe – an Atlaan flying machine – which will automatically set a course to the pyramid. Let us prepare for our journey.'

Susan and Roger felt excited, but Susan noticed that there was a worried look on her father's face.

* * *

The cousins could not help feeling a pang of fear as the dark shape of the tapu mountain seemed to drop from beneath them. As they continued to gaze down through the transparent bottom of the spherical aircraft they saw twinkling clusters of lights which marked the positions of New Zealand towns. These became fainter and fainter as the earth receded, while above them in the black sky stars grew brighter and the Milky Way appeared like a vast arch of crushed crystal.

'Look, Sue, I can see the curve of the earth,' cried Roger as a silver glow above the horizon heralded the moonrise.

'The earth only seems to be falling away from us,' the professor explained. 'From what I understand from Neerak an Atlaan Cosmic Energy device reduces the pull of gravity on the Aerial Globe, allowing it to rise and float in the stratosphere while the earth revolves beneath it, then it descends to its destination. There is nothing like it in our technology.'

His words were true enough. When they had first seen it the children were reminded of a giant plastic balloon. It was completely round and they could easily see through its curved walls. Inside they had found comfortable couches on the transparent floor, while in the upper part of the globe floated strangely shaped and coloured blocks of Plaax which were the "engines" enabling it to defy gravity.

They had loaded boxes of supplies through a circular opening in the side, puzzling Roger because he had seen no sign of a door to close it with. He had also wondered how they were going to launch it from an underground pyramid.

When the stores had been safely stacked on the glass-like floor, the Atlaan girl had told them to make themselves comfortable on the couches which automatically moulded themselves to the shape of their bodies.

'Are you ready?' Neerak had asked, holding a black rod which appeared to be all that was needed to control the craft. 'There is no need to worry, the air will remain fresh and will be heated when necessary.' She had touched the rod and suddenly the circular doorway had disappeared. The entrance had seemed to magically fuse together.

Seeing Roger's look of surprise, Neerak had said 'This Globe is built from Plaax, the material which comes from energy. It can be caused to change its shape and texture by altering the energy fields surrounding it.' For Roger the words "energy fields" conjured up a mental image of the patterns of iron filings round a magnet which he knew from experiments at the school lab.

The Globe had begun to ascend slowly. As it did so the ceiling above it had seemed to melt away, and the next moment the four passengers had felt themselves pressed into their couches as the strange aircraft accelerated skywards. Looking down at the darkened mountain Roger had seen a patch of light shrinking as the opening through which they had flown closed to conceal the Time Pyramid.

As they had continued to soar Susan had noticed that Neerak looked sad.

'What is it?' she had asked her softly.

'I was thinking of the other pyramids which are no more,' Neerak had answered. 'They must have been destroyed by earthquakes or crushed by glaciers during an ice age. Perhaps some primitive people managed to enter and destroy some.'

'That's possible,' said the Professor. 'Ancient peoples in both Egypt and South America constructed pyramids. Perhaps the inspiration for this form of building came from your Time Pyramids.'

This information had not cheered Neerak in any way, and Susan had said hurriedly: 'Do you know who will be in the Antarctic pyramid?'

Neerak had shaken her head.

'I was the first to be put into the trance so I do not know into which pyramids the others were placed. It will be good if we find the Sleeper to be a young man called Gifon, but that would be expecting too much . . .'

Meanwhile, the motion of the Globe had ceased and it hung in space, miles above a vast layer of cloud which looked like a silver sea in the moonlight

'We have to wait now while the earth revolves and then at the right moment the Globe will descend at an angle to bring it close to the pyramid,' Neerak continued. 'Perhaps you would like to eat some of the food you brought, or you could sleep. We are going to be very busy later on.'

Susan curled up comfortably on her couch, the clear walls giving her the sensation of floating among the stars.

'When I was little I imagined this is how a wind fairy would feel flying in the night sky,' she murmured to Roger.

He gave a snort of laughter.

'You believe in fairies?' he teased. 'And pixies and elves? Ha! Ha!'

Susan turned her face away from him.

'Sometimes I think you have no nice feelings,' she said. 'What's wrong with fairies? I'll bet you believed in Santa as long as you got presents from him. Anyway, I think this whole business is more far-fetched than fairies.'

And, as he dropped off to sleep, Roger had to admit to himself that there was truth in what she said.

They were awakened by a low hissing sound as the Globe descended gently earthwards. Below them clouds spread from horizon to horizon like a desert of untidy cotton wool.

'Where do you think we're going to land, Daddy?' Susan asked.

'From the position of the red light on Neerak's earth model I should say the pyramid is on the ice plateau near the South Pole,' her father replied. 'That would be the area reached by Shackleton in 1909. It's over 10,000 feet high there . . .'

'But why haven't some explorers come across it?' Roger wanted to know.

'Antarctica covers four-and-a-half million square miles and only a fraction of that has been seen by Man, so it's not surprising that it has remained undetected. The ice cap is thousands of feet thick – if it melted the sea level would rise and flood the world – and the Time Pyramid may be buried under that great weight of ice.'

'I don't know how we'll reach it if it is,' Roger said.

'I'm sure Neerak will have some gadget to help,' Susan replied.

The Professor gazed down on the rumpled cloud below them and said: 'There must be foul weather under that cover.'

The sunlight reflecting from the white cloud carpet made the travellers screw up their eyes until Neerak touched her rod and the walls took on the colour of sunglasses. The Globe trembled slightly as it entered the thicker atmosphere, then they were passing through layers of vapour with the vibration increasing as the spherical craft slowed. A howling, freezing wind buffeted it as they broke through the cloud bank, ice particles pattered against the sides and frequently snow swirled about it.

In the white confusion the four people could feel the Globe hover, drop and hover again as though it was seeking a landing place. Then there was a bump and they found themselves partly buried in a snow drift.

'We'll have to wait for the blizzard to blow itself out. before we can get out and explore.' Professor White said.

Neerak nodded.

'No wonder my people thought the poles fit only for robots.'

They relaxed on their couches, eating ham sandwiches and apples. It was a strange experience for them to be warm and comfortable in a transparent bubble while all around them raged a polar storm. Snow fell on the Globe, but the warmth from within melted the flakes almost immediately. To his alarm Roger noticed that it was also melting beneath them and that their craft was gradually sinking.

'We'll be buried in a little while,' he warned the others.

'Don't be afraid,' said Susan. 'This is a flying machine and Neerak will just raise it before it goes down too far. Fancy not realizing that!'

The boy lay on his couch in a slightly sulky

silence, he was starting to feel bored. He began to doze while Neerak, followed by Susan, went up to the clear floor above where, beside the strange shapes of the anti-gravity motors, a streak of red light glowed within a cube of Plaax.

'That indicates where the Time Pyramid lies,' she explained. 'Once the blizzard dies down all we have to do is follow the direction it is pointing and we will find it.'

Susan gazed into the savage white world outside the Globe and thought of the explorers such as Amundsen, Captain Scott and Shackleton who had braved it on foot. When she had learned about them at school she had not given them much thought and only now realized the hardship they had had to put up with.

'We may have to wait some time,' Neerak said as they descended to the main floor. 'Shall we have some music?'

'Please,' said Susan, remembering the music she had been thrilled by when she first entered the Time Pyramid. Immediately the Globe was filled with soothing sounds which made her think of sunsets and waves breaking on tropical shores.

'How did you do that?'

Neerak laughed.

'By what your father calls telepathy,' she explained. 'My people made some machines which were controlled by human thought waves, usually devices for entertainment'

Susan sighed. Sometimes she wished she had been born in Atlaan times – before the robots revolted of course – and she dozed off thinking how nice it would be to be able to change the channels of a television set by merely thinking about it.

Roger was dreaming he was back at Harrow. He was at the house of his friend Paul, playing with a super Scalextric set. His red Ferrari was just overtaking Paul's green Mini when he felt a hand shaking his shoulder. He opened his eyes to see his uncle bending over him.

'Wake up, old chap,' said the Professor. 'The blizzard is over and it's time to go to the pyramid.' He pointed through the curving wall of the Globe. At first Roger was only aware of a pale blue sky overhead, then by following the line of the out-stretched finger he saw what appeared to be a triangular-shaped hill sparkling with ice.

'Is that . . .?'

'That must be the tip of it,' cried Susan, struggling into a bulky snow suit which had been brought from the Time Pyramid. 'Hurry up, Roger, we're ready to go.'

When all were dressed in overalls which Neerak explained were kept warn by Cosmic Energy devices, the Globe wall opened and polar air flooded in to chill their unprotected faces. They linked themselves to a long rope, scrambled out and began to trek across the frozen snow which crunched crisply beneath their feet. After a few minutes they reached the top of the pyramid which rose about fifty feet above them.

'Please clear the ice here,' said Neerak, pointing to one of the sloping sides. The Professor began to swing a light pick and soon slabs of ice were falling away. After a few minutes enough was removed to show silvery metal in which was the outline of a now familiar triangular door.

Neerak touched its apex with her control rod, which reminded Susan of a magic wand, and immediately the door slid upwards to reveal a sloping passage. Untying the safety rope the Atlaan girl entered, saying: 'Have no fear of hidden traps this time, they have been made safe automatically.'

They followed her inside and as in the first Time Pyramid they were enveloped by white gas, which destroyed any minute organisms which could be harmful to the Sleeper. Through a second door they found themselves on a gallery looking down on a great three-sided hall through which welcoming music swelled.

Without a word Neerak pointed to the centre of the floor – the crystal case which should have held the Sleeper's body was gone.

8 The Memory Mirror

'Something has awakened the Sleeper, but what could it be?' Susan cried.

'Could he have been woken up by himself?' Roger asked.

'I do not see how,' said Neerak. 'But perhaps after I was put into the trance the Masters developed a system which automatically caused the other Sleepers to wake if one was roused. It would be a logical idea.'

'Let's split up and search the pyramid,' Professor White suggested. 'I doubt if he would have willingly gone out into the cold. If he is alive he must be here somewhere.'

Neerak looked sorrowful and for a moment it seemed that tears would flow from her green eyes.

'If he lives he would have come to greet us when he heard the music,' she said. 'I did hope that at least one other Atlaan had survived. You have all been very kind to me but . . . but you are still strangers. I had been hoping that I would have found a young man here . . .' To everyone's surprise Neerak suddenly blushed. 'His name was Gifon. We were very fond of each other.'

Susan felt sudden relief. If Neerak had been in love with someone in her own time it was not so likely that she and Susan's father would be attracted to each other. Although Susan liked Neerak, she did not want her to take her mother's place even though her parents had separated.

'I'll search this gallery,' the Professor said in a businesslike voice. 'Neerak, you'd better take the main floors and you kids go down to the rooms beneath it'

They set off walking between the domes which contained machines more wonderful than anything known in their twenty-first century. Roger noticed there were differences between this pyramid and Neerak's.

'I suppose they improved the design as they went along,' he said.

Susan nodded, not particularly interested.

'I'll bet he's dead,' she said at last. 'I'll bet he was woken . . .accidentally and something went wrong and he crawled off to die somewhere.' She shivered.

They found themselves in a long hall. At the far end a large golden object, shaped like a dunce's cap, was mounted on a low platform with steps leading up to it. At the bottom of these steps a figure was huddled in an unnatural position, rather like a broken doll.

'There he is,' shouted Roger and ran across the shiny black floor. When he reached the body he saw it was a handsome young man dressed in a metallic blue tunic. Long hair – the same silvery shade as Neerak's – framed his deathly white face. A trickle of dried blood ran from the mouth down the neck.

'Is he dead?' gasped Susan, who had gone pale herself.

'I don't know,' said Roger, trying to find the pulse in the stranger's wrist. 'He's very cold. Run and get the others.'

Susan sped away, thankful to leave Roger with the body.

A minute later Neerak came racing down the hall, closely followed by the broad figure of Professor White.

'Gifon! Gifon!' she cried, and then burst into a language which the children guessed was Atlaan. She knelt beside the sprawled body, holding his hands and this time a tear did run down her cheek. Then she turned to the others.

63

'We must take him to the healing machines at once. Help me to carry him.'

The Professor bent down and managed to lift the body by himself. Neerak led the way to a small room in the centre of which was an oblong box of clear Plaax, similar to the one in which Gifon had lain in his long trance. Beside it were cubes of pearly material, balanced on each other. Once Gifon was placed in the box, Neerak touched a control and each cube glowed with a different colour. She breathed a deep sigh of relief.

'He lives – the colours prove that. Whether the machine can save him is another matter. At the moment it is making its diagnosis, then the treatment will begin.'

As she spoke the cubes began changing colour rapidly and a heavy greenish gas flowed about Gifon almost as though it was a liquid.

'When will we know whether he is going to be all right?' Susan asked.

'It'll take many hours,' answered Neerak. 'The colour patterns show that the brain has been damaged. He has been struck on the head violently and there is a chance that even the healing machine will not be able to save him.'

Professor White looked with wonder at the body lying in its bath of gas. He was awed by the thought of the benefit to the world when medical scientists could examine the machine and mass produce it. It could mean the end of disease on earth!

As he watched the gas changed colour and Gifon's chest began to rise and fall slightly and his face did not seem so bloodless. Suddenly a new thought occurred to the Professor and he woke from his daydream.

'Listen, Neerak,' he said. 'Unless Gifon had a fall – which is unlikely – he must have been attacked. That means . . .'

' . . . that there is an enemy in the Time Pyramid,'

chimed in Roger, hastily looking over his shoulder.-

'But who could it be?' said Susan. 'Who could have found the pyramid in the middle of Antarctica, entered it, woken Gifon and then hit him over the head?'

'It is a mystery we must solve quickly,' Neerak declared. 'There is perhaps more at stake than the life of poor Gifon. Remember I told you that when the Sickness fell on my people they were realizing their greatest dream.'

'You mean time travel,' said Roger.

'Yes. Before I went into the trance they had only got so far as simple experiments, but afterwards they must have had greater success. That golden cone by which we found Gifon is a time machine.'

'So he might have been about to embark on a time journey when he was struck,' hazarded the Professor.

'Or perhaps he had just returned from one. The Atlaans' fear about time travel was that if the past was tampered with it could alter the present.'

'I can see that,' said Roger. 'If a time traveller had suddenly appeared in the middle of the Battle of Hastings it could have changed history. The Normans might have thought it was an omen or a miracle and run away and Harold might have remained King, and the whole history of England could have been different. Supposing Gifon went back and affected history even in a tiny way . . .'

'We might not exist any more,' cried Susan. 'If the Battle of Hastings had been different perhaps one of our ancestors would have been killed and therefore not had any children, and the whole chain of people leading down the centuries to us would not have existed.'

'Sometimes very trivial incidents have altered the whole course of history,' said the Professor. 'In 637 a great battle was fought at Kadessia between the Arabs and the Persians. It lasted for three days, the armies retiring under a truce at nightfall and continuing the next day. Just before sunset on the third day the Persian general Rustam attacked the Arabs with his thirty-three war elephants. As they advanced on the terrified Arabs, one elephant went mad. It raced up and down between the two armies, completely out of control. Suddenly it turned and charged through the Persian ranks, spreading terror and confusion with the other elephants charging behind it. The Arabs seized their chance and attacked the disorganized Persians with the result they had a victory which affected world history. How different life might have been today if the mad elephant had charged in the other direction.'

'I'm sure that is very interesting,' said Neerak impatiently. 'But we must find out what happened to Gifon. Perhaps the Memory Mirror can tell us.'

'The Memory Mirror?' said Roger.

'That is what our Masters of Medicine called it. You will soon see why.' She crossed the room to where a row of complicated-looking pieces of apparatus stood, and wheeled one across to the healing machine. It was a strange contraption made up from the usual cubes of Plaax with a piece of material like black glass raised above it.

'Everything that happens to a human being is recorded in the memory section of the brain,' she explained. 'Of course we cannot consciously remember it all because it would be too big a strain on the mind. The Masters invented the Memory Mirror in order to see what was stored in a person's memory, and it was very useful for learning to understand mental illness.'

From the machine she took a bowl attached to a lead and gently placed it on Gifon's head like a helmet.

'We will go back to the moment he was awakened,' Neerak said as she bent over the control panel. 'It may take a little time, but we can speed up the process until we find the parts which are important'

'It's rather like replaying a television video tape,' said the Professor. Zig-zags of light flickered across the black screen and then changed to a dim grey shade.

'That must be the point where he is just beginning to come out of the trance,' said Neerak excitedly. 'I remember it was like that when you awakened me. See, he is regaining consciousness quickly.'

They watched fascinated as the screen changed and images began to form, blurred at first but soon becoming sharper. They were seeing what Gifon had seen as he came back to life, the sides of the case which melted away and then the three-sided roof of the pyramid above him.

'He is properly awake now,' Neerak said. 'Look!'

She drew a sharp breath as the screen showed a vague figure, then outstretched arms came into focus.

'He's being helped up,' said Susan. 'But who by?'

There was a close-up of the figure now and they could see its face. Neerak touched a control and the moving picture froze while she gazed at the screen intently.

'I cannot understand it,' she murmured as they all looked at the fine features with intense dark eyes and the silver-blond hair of the Atlaans cut in a straight fringe just above the eyebrows. 'I do not recognize that person as one of the Sleepers, yet he is an Atlaan all right.'

'Could they have put an extra person in the Time Pyramid at the last moment?' Professor White asked.

'I cannot tell. Perhaps we will learn more as we go on. I regret that the Memory Mirror can only show us what the subject saw, not what he said or heard. Look.'

As she spoke the screen showed a swaying view of the interior of the pyramid as seen by Gifon when he struggled to his feet. Sometimes the four watchers saw the other man, sometimes just his arms as he helped the Sleeper to walk after his trance which had spanned thousands of years. Finally the screen clouded and became dull grey, showing only occasional images.

'Now he sleeps,' explained Neerak. 'I wonder;

who that other man could have been. Oh, look . . .'

Among the jumbled pictures flickering on the Memory Mirror there was suddenly an image of Neerak's face, looking slightly younger and more beautiful than she really was.

'Dear Gifon,' she cried. 'He was dreaming of me. But we must go forward.' She touched a control and the pictures speeded up until the screen showed only flashing lights. When Neerak slowed the images down again they saw views of the Time Pyramid's galleries as seen by Gifon when he wandered about. Then they saw the stranger, speaking with an expression of determination on his face.

'It looks as though he is arguing about something,' said Susan.

'We had better move forward again,' said Neerak. 'I fear there is something evil about that man.'

When the next sequence of pictures slowed they saw a corridor which was familiar to the children.

'Gifon seems to be running into the hall where we found him,' said Roger. Images continued to appear on the screen like a cinema film, showing the stranger close to the cone-shaped time machine. At times the picture moved rapidly from side to side as though Gifon was shaking his head in answer to something the stranger was saying.

'I am sure they are talking about the Time Cone,' said Neerak. 'Now the stranger is climbing inside it, Gifon is moving forward – he is trying to stop him? Oh . . .'

The screen suddenly appeared to explode into whirling lights before going blank.

'That is where Gifon became unconscious,' said Neerak. 'It seemed as though he was struggling with the stranger.'

'I think he was trying to stop him using the machine,' said Roger.

'He must have gone on a time journey,' Neerak murmured as she switched off the Memory Mirror and removed the cap from Gifon's head.

'Then I must go after him and bring him back, there's no knowing what effect he might have on history,' said Professor White grimly. 'I am sure Gifon was attempting to stop him for that reason,'

'You are right, Simon,' agreed Neerak. 'We will travel to wherever he has gone. The Cone's controls should be set to take us to that point in time, though where it will be I cannot guess.'

'We're coming too,' cried Susan. 'I don't want to be left alone here.'

'That's right,' agreed Roger. 'If anything should go wrong it is best that we should be together.'

His uncle reluctantly agreed.

'We must go at once,' said Neerak. 'Gifon will be quite safe in the healing machine.'

They left the room and went to the hall where the golden Cone stood on its platform.

'There won't be room for us all in there,' said the Professor.

'We can only go one at a time,' said Neerak, examining symbols which were engraved on its side. 'This machine does not actually go into the past itself.'

The others looked puzzled.

'Of course I cannot explain how it works precisely, but the Cone creates a form of energy which is projected through time and reforms in a similar shape in the past or future. So one Cone can reproduce itself in a dozen different ages, or over and over again in the same age. Time travel had been held up for centuries because the energy could not be controlled, but just before I entered my pyramid a device was perfected. Called the Fokal it was a small wafer of Plaax which, when fitted into a time machine, channelled Cosmic Energy into different dimensions.'

Neerak now looked at the control panel which was mounted within the Cone.

'There will be no problem in going to its last destination,' she called. 'The controls appear to be set – which is lucky because I do not understand how to make it go to a particular time zone.'

'That's a pity,' whispered Roger to Susan, 'I'd have loved to see the Battle of Agincourt.'

'Or the Last Supper,' she said. 'Think of actually seeing Jesus –'

'One thing worries me,' interrupted the Professor. 'The surface of the earth may have altered dramatically over the last few thousand years, so the Cone might materialize within a solid mass. In the heart of a mountain, for example.'

'I understand the designers took care of that,' replied Neerak. 'The Cone can move in space as well as time, and it has sensors which make sure it will always remain above the surface of the ground. I think you should go first, Simon, then Roger and Susan and I shall go last because I have to work the control. All you have to do is sit inside the Cone and within seconds you will be transported.'

'All right,' said the Professor, stooping to enter the Cone. The circular door swung shut and patterns of light appeared to ripple down its walls. Neerak touched a control and the children watched with fascination as it began to vibrate slightly and emit a high-pitched bleeping sound. For a moment it shimmered and Roger fancied he could almost see through it, then it became solid again and the noise died away. Neerak opened the door and they saw that the Cone was empty. Susan had a sick feeling, it was too much like a conjuror's trick.

'Daddy would not even have had time to get out,' she exclaimed.

'He will be in a Cone identical to this one,' explained Neerak. 'He can get out of it in his own time. Each traveller has his own Cone in the new time zone so that he can always get back to the present if there is danger. Your turn, Roger.'

'Cheerio,' he said in a slightly shaky voice. 'See you in BC.'

He climbed into the Cone and closed the door after giving Susan a big wink to prove that he was not scared. Again the bleeping, the shimmer of light and then the Cone stood empty.

'He will be in his own time machine, too – like Daddy?' asked Susan doubtfully.

'That is right,' said Neerak. 'There is nothing to be afraid of. You should be with them in seconds, and then I shall join you.'

Susan stepped inside and hoped that the Atlaan girl would not notice that her legs were trembling slightly. As she sat on the simple seat she felt that this was far worse than when she waited for the jet plane to scream down the runway on her first flight. For one thing there had been over a hundred people in the aircraft – here she was going into the unknown by herself.

9 The Black Shore

It seemed to Susan she was rushing through a tunnel of darkness, a darkness so heavy it was almost solid about her. The Cone vibrated alarmingly and a great roaring filled her ears. There was another sound she was aware of and which took her several moments to recognize – it was herself crying out with fear.

She managed to stop and she sat very still while the sensation of hurtling through some endless night continued. She felt she was going faster and even faster and it made her hold her breath until she could feel her lungs aching. She hugged her arms about her. If only Daddy had been able to travel with her! When her father had gone in the Cone only a few seconds seemed to have lapsed before it was empty again, but Susan was sure minutes were passing. Then she thought, Minutes? Why, centuries must be passing!

She remembered that in some way she could not quite understand she was not in the Cone she had entered in the pyramid, but another . . . yet it seemed like the same one and she had not been aware of any change-over. Everything had become so odd since she and Roger had first entered the tunnel at the top of the *tapu* mountain. Gradually she began to lose the sensation of travelling at great speed, and through the walls of the Cone she saw a glow as though dawn was ending a very dark night. It grew brighter and brighter until she could see the colour of the dress over her knees, and then she realized she had arrived – at wherever it was she had arrived.

The Cone's walls had become transparent – no doubt the Atlaans had devised this so the time traveller could see if the area was safe before they got out – and Susan felt as though she was in an enormous soap bubble with rainbow colours shot through it. She looked about her. The Cone had come to rest on a beach of black sand, with a stretch of still water to one side and a line of low but steep cliffs to the other. Nothing moved, and there was certainly nothing to frighten her. But there was no sign of her Daddy or Roger.

Summoning up her courage she opened the door and stepped into a past world. The air was cool and it made her shiver slightly, and it also smelt different and caused her to breathe faster than normal. Later she understood this was because the world was much younger and there had not been time for vegetation to create as much oxygen in the atmosphere as she was used to. The sun was a large orange ball just above the horizon and it bathed the indigo sea and the dark coast with a ruddy glow. What surprised her most was the absolute silence, no breeze sighed, no wave lapped on the sand and no bird or animal uttered a cry. It seemed to be a dead world.

She took several steps forward and then looked back at the Cone. It stood looking just as solid as it did – or one like it – in the Time Pyramid, and Susan was pleased that its door remained open, suggesting that she could easily get back inside if she needed to.

I must have come a long way back through time, she thought, *because this beach has nothing to do with Antarctica. It must be before the earth changed its axis. But where can Daddy and Roger be, and Neerak, she should be here now.*

Suddenly she felt sick with loneliness, so sick that she had to sit down on the damp sand. Supposing they arrived at another point in time! They might be only separated by a few hours, yet those hours would be a bar

73

she could never cross. She might be lost in time, and it seemed much worse than when she got lost at the John Lewis' store in Oxford Street when she was a toddler. At least there had been plenty of people about then to take notice when she opened her mouth and bellowed, now it was possible she was the only human being on the whole earth.

'I mustn't panic,' she told herself firmly. 'I know I'm scared stiff at being on my own but that's no excuse to behave stupidly. Perhaps I should go along the shore.'

She spoke aloud, and the words sounded peculiar in her ears because of the brooding – almost evil – silence which hung over everything.

She looked up and down the shore, trying to decide which way to explore. Ahead of her it curved in the form of a wide crescent-shaped bay, with what appeared like low hills behind its cliffs. In the opposite direction the beach went straight for a mile and then ended where reddish cliffs fell straight down to the sea.

'I think I'll go towards the bay,' Susan said, 'but first . . .' From her pocket she took out her diary, and tearing out a page, wrote with its tiny pencil, 'Have gone along the shore looking for you – Love S.' Then she drew an arrow to make the message doubly clear and carefully placed the paper on the seat of the Cone.

This done she set off, bravely trying to whistle 'Rain-drops Keep Falling on my Head'. In the pocket of her anorak she fingered a bar of chocolate and then decided it would be wiser to leave it until she was really hungry.

Every so often she would pause and look behind her. Apart from the time machine dwindling in size nothing changed, but the fact that she was getting further and further away from it added to her nervousness. Yet she knew that she must press on to try and find her father or Roger.

'I suppose I ought to be excited,' she said, 'After all, I must be one of the first few humans to travel back in time. It's like being one of the Moon astronauts in a way. But I wish it was more interesting. I'm glad there are no prehistoric monsters of course, but a few trees or some birds would be nice. Perhaps I've gone back before the development of birds – or even life . . .'

At that moment she heard the first sound, other than her own voice, since she had arrived on the black shore. It was a noise like the gurgling of water going down a plug-hole magnified a thousand times. Susan turned towards the oily sea and saw a snake-like neck rearing about twenty feet above the surface. There was a flat, ridiculously small head at the top of it, with dull eyes and a gash for a mouth. From it hung a long strand of grey-brown seaweed which waved as the great neck swayed to and fro like a sapling in a gale.

Susan watched fascinated, and was rather relieved that the creature appeared to be a vegetarian. Then she noticed a ripple nearby and another flat head appeared and rose on a tall neck. It swung towards the other head, its jaws agape. At first Susan thought it was going to attack, but it was only interested in the seaweed. The first creature shook its head and swayed away, determined not to share the food, but the second swooped towards it and seized the other end. Susan, forgetting her fear and the strangeness of the prehistoric world she had only just entered, almost burst out laughing as a tug of war developed. Both necks arched as each animal tried to wrest the long frond of weed from the other. Sometimes their heads were close to the water, sometimes they stretched to a height which made Susan wonder what size their submerged bodies must be. And as the contest continued both creatures snorted and gurgled as though they were enjoying a game.

Suddenly the game changed.

Susan saw a long ripple moving towards them at high speed. It reminded her of the wake of a torpedo she had once seen in a war film. When it had almost reached the two playful monsters it changed into a fury of foam.

One of the creatures suddenly released the seaweed, its neck straightened as tall as a mast and from its mouth came a continuous shriek. For a moment it reared and Susan saw a black glistening body break the surface. In its side was a long gash from which crimson liquid pumped in regular spurts. Then the girl saw something else beside it, something with glittering scales about its short neck and enormous head – a head which had to be enormous to have such a mouth filled with rows of dagger teeth.

A second later these terrible jaws closed on the base of the vegetarian's neck. The scream ended suddenly, the neck crumpled into a despairing arch and the barrel body sank beneath the slick of its own blood. Then, with its eyes turned upwards to the sky, the head slipped from sight.

The other beast had turned and was fleeing through the water with the weed still drooping from its mouth, its neck making a bow wave like that of a yacht. Again there was the torpedo ripple behind it, and suddenly it too began to shriek and thresh the water as the underwater hunter caught up with it.

Susan turned away, not wishing to see the grim climax to the drama. Tears began to roll down her cheeks as she thought of the dreadful fate which had so suddenly overtaken the two playful animals. When she looked out to sea again the surface was as glassy as before, only a dark stain marked the scene of the drama.

Praying that the predator was incapable of coming ashore, Susan crossed the wide expanse of black sand and kept close to the perpendicular cliffs. She kept looking anxiously to where the sun was almost touching the rim of the sea. She had made up her mind that before it sank she would return to the Cone for safety, the thought of being out in the prehistoric night was too horrible to think of. First she wanted to reach the far end of the bay in the hope that beyond it she would see the Cones which had brought her father and her cousin.

Thinking of Roger she wished she had been less irritable with him at times, though she had to admit that he was an annoying boy. But at that moment she felt she could forgive him anything just to hear the sound of his voice or his shy laugh.

She passed the opening of a large cave in the cliff from which a stream carved a runnel through the sand. She bent down and tested the water and found it to be pure. After taking several gulps of it from her cupped hands she straightened up and caught sight of a movement in the dark depths of the cavern.

'I mustn't start imagining things simply because I saw those poor creatures attacked,' she muttered to herself as she crunched along the shore. 'I'm sure I have come back to the time when all life lived in the sea – I hope I have come back to the time when all life lived in the sea.' But she could not help looking over her shoulder, and there was something coming out of the cave – something dark in the dramatic light of the dying sun, something that leapt up and down reminding her of a kangaroo. It was hard to see exactly what it was. It looked like a large sack with a narrow head and powerful hind legs that propelled it along in a series of bounces.

Susan broke into a run, the coarse black sand filling her shoes unpleasantly. She looked behind again, and saw that the hopper was coming in the same direction.

Oh dear, it's after me, she thought. *Kangaroos only eat grass, but is it a kangaroo? There's no grass here!*

The thin air made her heart beat painfully as she

ran faster, and each time she cast a glance behind it seemed that the unknown thing was getting closer.

At last she could run no more. She halted, sobbing for air, and leaned against the rough face of the cliff. The hopper continued towards her as though it had springs instead of legs. It made a shrill squeaking sound. Susan looked round wildly for a weapon, but there was nothing, not even a stone or a piece of driftwood on the sand. She felt in her pocket and her fingers closed on the sticky bar of chocolate. For a moment she had the crazy notion that it might leave her in peace if she offered it some.

As it bounded closer she saw the flash of pointed teeth, glittering eyes and long claws on its forelegs. It squeaked louder and louder . . .

10 Winged Fury

'Get away, you horrid brute!'

Susan almost laughed with relief as she recognized the voice. The hopper paused, swivelling its wicked eyes and squeaking in surprise at the unexpected sound.

'Go on, scram!' A stone thudded into the sand close to the animal. It was followed by another which struck it on the rump. The hopper was so startled it fell over, floundered back onto its hind legs and began leaping back along the shore, while a third stone went whistling after it to help it on its way.

Susan moved back from the cliff and looked up. There, outlined against the rosy sky, was Roger.

'All right, Sue?' he called.

She nodded, too relieved to speak for a moment.

'You shouldn't encourage animals like that, they might not be friendly.'

'I never,' she cried and then laughed, realizing that dear old Roger was teasing her.

'Walk along the beach a bit more and you'll come to a place where, the cliff is not so steep. You can climb up there. And leave the local wildlife in peace.'

She followed his instructions and set off along the beach. He kept pace with her on the cliff top, chatting in a loud voice to keep her spirits up although she didn't need it now she was no longer alone in this frightening world.

'I worked out that we arrived in different places because of earth spin,' he said. 'It's something we did not take into account As we left at intervals of a few seconds

79

we arrived at points a few miles apart. Now I have seen where your Cone is, I can work out where your father's should be.'

'How?'

'If we take a line from your Cone to mine, his must be further along it You can climb up here, I'll give you a hand.'

Susan scrambled up a slope where the rock face had collapsed, and Roger reached down to help her up the steep part. Next moment he put his arms round her and gave her the first hug he had ever given her in his life.

'Darling old Sue,' he laughed. 'Am I glad to see you! Until I reached the cliff and saw your Cone in the distance I thought I was alone in the Mesozoic Age.'

When the first excitement of the reunion was over Susan looked about her and realized that she was on the edge of a plain which stretched eastwards to a line of ragged mountains on the horizon. Beneath her feet there was reddish clay, the same hue as the cliffs she had followed. Nowhere was there a blade of grass, a flower or any plants with leaves which fell with the seasons. Nearby drooped low clumps of drab-coloured ferns, and beyond them patches of shrubby bushes.

'Even the vegetation seems to be very primitive,' Roger said. 'It's odd, I was doing a project on prehistoric times at school a couple of terms ago. Only wish I had a camera. People would think we were mad if we told them all about this and did not have any photographs to prove it. Look at the lovely colours of those mountains.'

In the slanting rays of the sun the distant peaks were the most colourful things in the silent world. They glowed red, white, ochre and delicate pink, reminding Susan of pictures she had seen of the Grand Canyon.

'Look over there, by that group of dead trees, you'll see my Cone,' said Roger as they came to the top of a gentle rise. 'Now if yours is over there, a line from it to mine would point in that direction . . . so we must head towards the tallest peak in the range and I'll bet we come across uncle.'

'I hope we find him before dark, the sun's very low.'

'Yes, but since I've been here I have noticed that it doesn't seem to get much lower. It moves much more slowly than the sun we were used to.'

'Let's start then, the sooner we find Daddy the better. He must be worried sick about us.'

Hand in hand they set off across the clay plain. Occasionally they waded waist deep through belts of bushes which reminded them of stunted conifers. Several times they had to cross deep gullies which, when it rained, would drain the water from the flat landscape.

'Like some chocolate?' Susan asked when they halted for a rest at the bottom of one of these which still held a few pools of stagnant water from the last downpour. 'It's melting in my pocket so we may as well eat it now.'

'Good old Cadbury's Dairy Milk,' said Roger as he removed the blue and gold wrapper. 'This could be the first bit of litter in the history of the world. I'll bet no one at the factory ever dreamed it would travel back in time millions and millions of years . . .'

'Millions and millions?'

'Yes, the Mesozoic Age came to an end nearly a couple of hundred million years ago.'

'Oh dear.'

'What difference does it make – a few hundred years or many million. It's probably better that we've come to a time without people. Imagine if we'd materialized only three or four centuries ago – we'd have been burnt at the stake as witches: So far this time zone seems fairly safe.'

'You should have seen what I saw on the beach. I

wonder why the stranger in the Time Pyramid wanted to come back here anyway.'

'It's a mystery, and I think it'll be hard to find him now. Perhaps Neerak'll know how to locate him. For a woman she's very clever.'

'How dare you say "for a woman" . . .?' And they began to argue as they crossed the flat bed of the gully. At that moment Roger noticed a distant shadow flitting across the ground, reminding him of the shadow cast by the helicopter at the Ronsons' sheep station. He glanced up to see a large shape black against the sky. It seemed clumsy compared to a modem bird, especially when it flapped its ungainly wings, but when it held them still it flew like a glider and with the same speed.

'A pterodactyl!' he cried. 'Watch out, it seems to be following us!'

They watched as the creature circled high above them.

'It looks like a kite that's broken away from its string,' said Susan as it began to swoop earthwards. She clung to Roger's arm, but he did not notice the pressure of her fingers. He could not take his eyes off the flying reptile which not so long ago he had been drawing for his school project. He saw that it had a bird-shaped head, the body of a scaly animal and the rear legs of a lizard. Its bat-like wings stretched from long jointed fingers attached to its forelegs and, unlike a bird, its jaws were filled with teeth. From between these came a whistling sound.

Roger suddenly came to life and pulled Susan down behind a rock. The airborne lizard gave a hiss of rage as it sailed less than a yard above them, then it began to beat its wings furiously to gain height for the next attack. It rose in lumbering circles until its fifteen foot wingspan dwindled to a small triangular silhouette.

'Here it comes again,' whispered Susan.

'Keep well down.' said Roger. 'It's like a

prehistoric dive bomber.'

High above them the pterodactyl glided in a slow circle, positioning itself to make the next attack. Then it began its swift descent. To Roger it was like something out of a nightmare but he knew that, unlike the Mist Lizard, it was not a creation of his own imagination.

He pressed Susan down further behind the rock and as he did so he saw a golden figure standing on the lip of the gully. He held an object which reminded the boy of an old fashioned blunderbuss with a square mouth. As the pterodactyl came whistling towards the children the stranger raised it to his shoulder and from it streaked something silver, a metallic insect thing which hummed through the air like an enraged dragonfly. It took a curving course to meet the reptile which gave a shriek of dismay and then vanished in a flash of white flame. Charred fragments of its wings spiralled to the ground, leaving trails of oily smoke behind them.

The figure lowered his weapon and waved encouragingly to the children, calling words which they could not understand.

'It's the man from the Time Pyramid,' gasped Susan. 'We've found him.'

'You mean – he's found us. And very lucky for us, too.' They crossed the gully floor and scrambled up the bank where he was waiting to meet them, a calm look on his handsome features. He wore a tunic which seemed to have been woven from fine golden wire, and the blunderbuss was now slung across his broad shoulders by a strap.

He held out his hand in a sign of friendship and Roger shook it, thanking him for destroying their enemy even though he knew the man could not understand him. Then he took out his pocket knife and began scratching marks on the hard clay. First he drew a rough Time Cone – whereupon the stranger nodded – then two stick people and pointed to Susan and himself. Then he drew two more and pointed in the direction of the pink peak they had been following. Again the man nodded and waved his hand as though inviting Roger to lead the way.

'I wonder how he found us,' whispered Susan as they resumed their trek across the plain. She was rather overawed by the tall man who strode so easily beside them in calm silence.

That's it – he's too calm, she thought. *Not at all like somebody who would hit Gifon over the head!*

They walked for another half hour and then, breaking through a screen of shrivelled bushes, they saw a Time Cone and standing beside it was Professor White and Neerak.

It seemed strange to Susan to be drinking warm sweet tea in the Mesozoic Age. Her father had just poured it from his Thermos flask, and now he was rummaging in his pack for a packet of sandwiches. They were a bit stale, having travelled all the way from the New Zealand Time Pyramid, but the children wolfed them down, suddenly very hungry after their adventures.

They had learned that Neerak's Cone had arrived further along the beach from Susan's, but she had been able to easily calculate where the first one would be and had headed straight for it. Roger looked up from his food and saw the Atlaan girl deep in conversation with the stranger.

'He has an amazing gun, uncle,' he said. 'It fires a sort of metal insect. It homed in on the pterodactyl like a living thing and then blew it up in a great flash of fire.'

'Then we'd better be careful not to get on the wrong side of him,' said the Professor with a slight laugh. "I notice that Neerak seemed a little nervous of him.'

'Have you any idea who he might be, Daddy?' Susan asked.

'No, I expect Neerak will tell you soon. It's hard to understand why he should harm Gifon and later save you two.'

A few minutes later Neerak came over to them, leaving the stranger by the Cone, watching the colours of the mountain range deepen as the sun finally set

'His name is Metnal,' said Neerak as she sat down beside them. 'He is an Atlaan but I am puzzled as I have never seen him before.'

'But you couldn't have known everybody,' Roger said.

'No, but I knew all those who were to become Sleepers. We trained together. According to his story he was selected at the last minute, some time after I had been put into the trance. He had been in space and therefore had escaped the Sickness, and only returned to earth in time to be placed in the last pyramid with Gifon.

'He explained that a system had been developed so that if one Sleeper was awakened the others would be automatically revived. He says he woke all right, but found Gifon must have suffered some mental disturbance during his trance. Apparently Gifon was under the illusion that Metnal was some evil creature and wanted to kill him.'

The Professor recalled the images he had seen on the screen of the Memory Mirror.

'I suppose that could be so,' he said a little doubtfully. 'Gifon did seem to be chasing him, and there was a sort of struggle at the end.'

'Certainly the Gifon I knew would not have harmed anyone,' said Neerak, 'but who can say how the trance might have affected his mind. Metnal said that in order to escape from Gifon he climbed into the Cone after knocking him down. He pressed the control and found himself back in this age.'

'It sounds a straightforward story,' mused Roger. 'I

suppose if you were being chased by someone who was out to kill you it would be logical to use the Cone to escape.'

Neerak said nothing for a while.

'I suppose it is the truth,' she admitted at last. 'It is just that I cannot believe that my – that Gifon could have changed so much.

'I can't help thinking that Metnal hardly looks the type to run away,' Professor White added.

'He said that he intended to go back only a few hours so that Gifon would still be in his trance but he did not have a chance to set the controls properly. Tomorrow, when it is light, we can go back to our Cones and return to the twenty-first century, and then we will learn the truth.'

'Daddy, I'm very tired,' said Susan suddenly, 'I'd like to go to sleep.'

'Of course, you must be exhausted after your adventures,' he answered. She laid her head on his lap and almost immediately felt herself engulfed by a wonderful wave of sleep.

11 Marooned in Time

Roger opened his eyes and realized he was very cold and uncomfortable. He had been having a nightmare about the Mist Lizard. Now his mind wandered back over the chain of events which had led from the first adventure to his journey back through time. But if it was the present to him, it was still the dim distant past to people of the twenty-first century . . .

Suddenly he had an idea about time.

He imagined it like a cinema film which ran through a projector with everyone seeing its images on a screen. The Past was the film which had been shown, the Future was the film which was still on the reel, and the Present was that bit of film actually in the projector. Each person was like a projector living out their lives frame by frame, which did not make the past and future film any less real.

In some miraculous way the Cone had taken them back if to a very early part of the film, and now it was being re-run through the projector which was Roger. He was excited by the idea which in some ways he found very comforting. It meant that nothing was ever really lost. He wanted to explain it to Susan so he sat up and looked for her. She lay with her head still on her father's lap. Roger climbed swiftly to his feet. It was early morning in the Mesozoic Age and the thin air was chilly.

'Hello,' said Susan opening one eye. 'Oh Daddy, you must have been uncomfortable sitting like this through the night'

87

'That's what dads are for sometimes,' the Professor laughed. 'Somebody had to keep watch. Luckily I'm used to hard conditions through going on remote digs. I wonder what's happened to Neerak and Metnal.'

'Now it's light we'll be able to find our way back to our Cones and return to our own time,' said Susan. 'I used to criticize our world a lot, but it's a million times better than this dreary one.'

'Metnal's gone!' They looked round to see Neerak.

'I cannot find a trace of him,' she said. 'He must have vanished in the night.'

'You don't think some creature came . . .' said Susan with a shudder.

'Of course not, with that blunderbuss of his he'd be a match for anything,' Roger declared.

'He must have gone off exploring or something'

'He hasn't gone to one of the Cones to return to the twenty first century,' suggested the Professor.

Neerak shook her head. 'If he wanted to do that he could have taken this one. Why should he walk all the way to another – and in the dark? And why did he not tell me? Am I not one of his people?'

They sat in silence, completely puzzled by the disappearance. Roger got up and prowled about, looking for footprints but the reddish clay was too hard to take the imprint of shoes.

'Perhaps he's not gone very far,' said Professor White. 'He might have gone to some gully to – well, we all have to go off by ourselves at times.'

Neerak shrugged impatiently.

'It is not that. I have called him with my mind. It was something we could all do in my time. What do you call it again, Simon?'

'Telepathy.'

'Yes, I have called him by telepathy and there was no response. I think he must be dead, or unconscious. His conscious mind is not functioning.'

'Perhaps these are not the right conditions for telepathy. After all, it is a very different world to the one you are used to.'

'Perhaps, but I must search for him. He must have had some accident.'

'If we all spread out . . .' began Roger.

'No,' said Neerak. 'You children may go back to the Time Pyramid. I think it is too dangerous here. If it had not been for Metnal you would have both been pterodactyl food by now.'

'But . . .' protested Roger.

'Neerak is quite right,' said his Uncle.

'Susan can go now in this Cone,' said Neerak. 'When we reach the next one we'll send Roger. Once we've found out what has happened to Metnal we will join you.'

Susan kissed her father and climbed into the Cone with relief. Neerak touched the control to send it forward through time. For a moment she looked puzzled, then announced: 'The Cone is dead. It has no power. Come out Susan.'

They watched anxiously while the Atlaan girl carefully examined the controls within the Cone.

'The Fokal has gone,' she announced at length. 'Do you remember I explained that it converted Cosmic Energy to transmit the Cone through other dimensions? It is only a small block of Plaax – about the size of one of your chocolate bars – but it is essential. Here, you can see that the slot where it fitted is empty.'

'But what could have happened to it? asked Susan in a disappointed voice.

'Only Metnal would have known about the Fokal,' said Neerak. 'He has stolen it and left us stranded.'

* * *

The orange sun had risen in the prehistoric sky and

the plain was starting to shimmer with the heat. There was still no breeze to cool it, and the children trudged along with their anoraks slung over their arms. All morning they had been trekking in the direction of the distant mountains, the direction Neerak believed Metnal must have taken.

'He would not have gone back to the coast,' she argued. 'There would be nothing for him there. I can only believe that, for some reason, he wants to return to the Cone he came in, and he did tell me that it had materialized near the mountains.'

'He might have been lying to you,' said Roger. 'He seems a very unreliable person.'

'I cannot understand it, I am beginning to think that it is he who is mad and not poor Gifon. That could explain why I have no mental contact with him.'

Susan kept scanning the sky for pterodactyls but apart from two distant dots hovering in the direction of the black shore there was no sign of life.

'It seems to be a very empty world. Daddy,' she said as she walked beside her father.

'Most life was – er, is – probably still in the water,' he replied. 'The Mesozoic Age lasted one hundred and fifty-five million years, during which time dinosaurs developed and then died out, giving way to mammals. As you saw a pterodactyl I'd say we might be at the end of the Triassic period of the Mesozoic. Luckily there's not much vegetation on this plain so it cannot support any hungry dinosaurs. They're likely to be found in the lush swampy ground around lakes, like the Florida everglades in our own day.'

'But the landscape seems so empty and the colours of the trees are so drab. It's as though nature is just waiting.'

'It reminds me a bit of the Australian outback where I did some field work before you were born – a

90

great emptiness which has been waiting patiently for something to happen for millions of years. Quite uncanny, really. You feel as though you're trespassing.'

'That's just what I feel, and the sooner we find Metnal and get into the Cones and stop trespassing the better I shall like it.'

'Perhaps it's waiting for Man to come,' Roger said. 'In that case it'll have to wait quite a while. Man first appeared a hundred and seventy-eight million years after the Triassic period ended.' He looked rather smug over this information he had picked up through working on his school project. 'In a funny sort of way I rather like it here. It's like being in on a great mystery, at the very beginning of things.'

'You would,' said Susan. 'Anything awful like this you would like . . . If only you hadn't wanted to go up the *tapu* mountain.' And they began bickering, which helped to pass the time.

Every half hour the small party took a short rest, usually in a gully where there were shallow pools of water so they could drink. Roger was thankful that there was still food in his uncle's pack, but he knew it would not last. And then – if they had not found Metnal – what would they do?

Perhaps we are going to die here, he thought suddenly. *Our bones might even become fossilized. That would give some twenty-first century palaeontologist a fit if he found human remains in Mesozoic strata.*

As they approached the mountains the ground became undulating as though giant ripples had been formed when the range was thrown up. As they reached the top of one of these they gazed down into a shallow valley and saw the sun flickering on a golden object.

'It must be Metnal's Cone,' cried Roger and they raced down the slope towards it. When they reached the time machine there was no sign of life and Neerak quickly opened the circular door and climbed in. When she reappeared there was a look of disappointment on her usually calm features.

'The Fokal is missing,' she said. 'He has taken this one as well.'

'Look, there are footprints,' said Susan, pointing to the ground which was no longer hard but powdery like dry desert dust. 'They must be from when he first arrived,' her father remarked.

'No, uncle,' Roger said. 'Look at these sets. One track leads away from the Cone towards the mountains. I'm sure he must have come back here and taken the Fokal after he left us. For some reason he wants to prevent us getting back to our own tune.'

'I think he does not want us to see Gifon,' mused Neerak. 'He knows we would return to the pyramid.'

'He can only be a few hours ahead of us,' said the Professor. 'Let's get after him and see if you can talk some sense into him, Neerak.'

They pressed on, following the line of footprints over the red dunes.

'It looks as though he was heading for that,' said Neerak pointing to a V-shaped gap in the foothills of the multi-coloured mountains. Next moment they half slid down a steep bank, clouds of choking dust swirling about them.

'How I'd like to see some soil,' Susan cried. 'I never thought much about soil before, but now I think it's lovely stuff.'

'It hasn't evolved yet, I suppose,' said Roger.

'No grass, no flowers, no moss – just stupid old scrub and unpleasant trees without even proper leaves,' grumbled Susan.

'Come on Susie,' encouraged her father. 'We'll be at that valley soon and things may be better there. At least there'll be some shade. It's starting to heat up now the sun is getting higher.'

After another hour of trudging over unpleasantly soft dust, they found themselves on hard rock at the mouth of the valley. They could not see far along it because of a curve to the right, and much of it was in deep shadow. After the heat of the plain the four companions found it refreshingly cool and it was not long before they reached the corner.

Roger had run on ahead, anxious to see what was beyond it. The others saw him stop and stare at something out of their line of vision.

He turned to them and shouted: 'I can't believe it – there's a city . . .'

'Don't tease,' called Susan. But when they rounded a shoulder of pink and grey striped rock, they too stood still in amazement.

The valley widened out into a great flat-bottomed bowl several miles across and surrounded by steep mountains. In the centre of it there rose a collection of slim tower-like buildings which glittered like some magic palace in a fairytale. Filled with wonder, they began to walk towards it in silence, almost afraid that it would vanish before their eyes.

At last Roger spoke. 'You don't think it is a vision, I mean a sort of mirage which has come back from the future.'

'No,' said the Professor quietly. 'No mirage casts shadows.'

The slender buildings which rose so gracefully about a central tower were real enough. They were constructed of some milky-coloured substance shot with rainbow colours such as you see in oil splashes on a wet road. It reminded Susan of her mother's opal ring. The tops of the towers were pointed like those of medieval German castles. Below them were circular buildings connected by ramps, bridges and delicately spiralling flights of stairs.

'There's not a sign of life,' murmured Professor White. 'Neerak, have you any idea what this place could be?'

'It is not unlike the buildings the Atlaans used to construct,' she said slowly. 'But it could not have anything to do with them. Millions and millions of years will have to pass before men even built rough huts.'

'Perhaps there was a human race at the very beginning of time and which died out,' Roger mused.

'Rubbish,' said Susan.

'At least we know what Metnal was looking for,' said the Professor. 'Come on, we must explore.' And they continued their march towards the shining towers.

12 The Singing City

They approached the city almost fearfully, as though they expected that at any moment it would vanish and they would be left abandoned in a hostile world, but the towers and spires remained steel hard in the harsh sunlight. As they drew nearer they saw that it did not rise out of the rocky floor of the valley but from a base of silvery metal which at one point of its perimeter had a flight of steps in it.

'Listen,' cried Susan. A high-pitched humming issued from the city as though it contained magnificent machines which had spun into awesome life.

'The city's singing – it's alive,' she said.

'The city may be alive,' snorted Roger, 'but I'll bet there's nothing living there.'

'Apart from Metnal,' his uncle added. 'Come on, let's see what there is to be seen.' Roger and Susan could see that his archaeologist's curiosity had been set aflame. He led them up the steps and they found themselves on the flat platform on which the city stood. Between the opal buildings there were narrow walkways, while overhead there were arches and graceful flying buttresses.

Directly in front of the time-travellers was an open square. On each side there was a colonnade and at the far end was a large domed building which vaguely reminded Roger of pictures he had seen of the Taj Mahal. It had a large entrance – its solid metal door appeared to have been drawn up like a portcullis – and when they entered they found themselves in a round hall lit by cool light which, after the glare of the prehistoric noon, had a strange underwater atmosphere.

In the centre stood a pair of statues and a ray of light from the roof illuminated them like a spotlight. One was a grotesque figure which reminded the children of a deep-sea diving suit, except instead of an air-hose it had several branching antennae and instead of two arms it had four.

Beside this ugly figure was a carving of a tall man draped in a long cloak. He had fine calm features and he seemed to be looking up at the heavens while the 'diver' was gazing down at his enormous feet. The handsome man held his hand lightly on the shoulder of his companion. Neerak had given a gasp when she entered the hall and saw the two figures, and a moment later Susan thought she knew why the graceful figure was easy to recognize.

'It's Metnal,' she exclaimed.

'It certainly looks like him,' agreed her father. 'But what is that uncouth fellow beside him with the goggle eyes and the four arms?'

It reminds me of something I saw once in a history lesson when I was a child,' mused Neerak. 'But the other certainly resembles Metnal. I cannot understand this place.'

Puzzled, they left the hall and came to a building with a ramp running up to its roof.

'Let's go up there and well get a bird's eye view – I should say a pterodactyl's eye view – and we may see our elusive friend,' said Roger.

They began to climb the inclined path. There was no rail or balustrade and Roger, who had no head for heights, was soon sorry that he had made the suggestion. On the other hand Susan was not worried at all, and often stood on the very edge, looking down. It made Roger almost dizzy to see her, but he knew that if he said anything she would only tease him.

When they reached the flat roof they lost all interest in looking down on the city – before them was the most unlikely object they could have imagined, a brightly-coloured, old fashioned roundabout with carved horses beneath a canopy with fancy crimson letters, 'JASPER SUGGS FAIRGROUND ENTERTAINMENTS.'

It was baffling. Roger and Susan raced to the platform and climbed on to a couple of horses. Roger's was black with wild eyes and a silver mane, Susan's was a pretty white one covered with blue and gold stars. Almost immediately the platform began to revolve, the horses rose and fell accompanied by the sound of a steam organ blaring 'Swannee River'.

'What fun,' cried Susan as her horse plunged beneath her. 'I haven't been on one of these for ages – not since I went to the fair on Hampstead Heath.'

'It's super,' agreed Roger, and then he thought to himself, *Perhaps I've gone mad. What am I doing riding a merry-go-round in the middle of a deserted city in the Mesozoic Age? It just can't be happening to me.*

But it was. Faster and faster went the merry-go-round, louder and louder echoed the music and the horses leapt furiously as though they were being ridden in the Grand National.

Even Neerak and the Professor caught the children's enthusiasm, standing close to the platform and laughing as Roger and Susan appeared to be racing each other. Although Neerak had never seen a roundabout in her life she clapped her hands and shouted encouragement to the two riders. To Susan it seemed that she really was racing her cousin. When her horse rose his fell so that she could look down on him, then his black steed seemed to leap forward and it was her turn to look up.

'Faster! Faster!' she shouted as though she was a very small girl again.

'Come on Black Bess,' urged Roger. 'We've got to get to York!'

The platform began to slow, the music faltered and the horses moved less and less – then there was silence and without a word, Susan climbed down. Everything had become so topsy-turvy that she hardly knew what to say or how to act. Had they done wrong in enjoying themselves?

Roger stayed on his black mount. He had the odd feeling that by an effort of will he might have been able to force the horse to go faster and faster until it galloped through time itself back to his own age, and he would have found himself on a fairground roundabout with everything having taken place in his imagination. But he did not have enough willpower and everything remained the same – utterly inexplicable.

Suddenly he pointed over the heads of the others and yelled, 'There's Metnal.'

They turned and saw the tall man in the golden tunic approaching them from the direction of the ramp. When he drew close he halted and spoke in Atlaan to Neerak who later translated his words for the others.

'I regret that I had to leave you but it was necessary,' he said.

'We feared that you were lost and hurt,' she replied. We searched for you, and for the Fokal for the Cone.'

'I needed it to bring this city to life,' he answered. 'Can you not hear it singing with its new found power?'

'Tell me, what is this place – and what do you have to do with it?'

'That would take too long now but I am master here. You must remember that and do what I command. I feel no ill will towards you, but neither would it trouble me if I had to kill you.'

As he spoke he raised his blunderbuss

meaningfully.

'But we come from the same time – we are both Sleepers, why do you threaten?' cried Neerak.

'It is necessary,' he answered as calmly as ever, though the others could sense the menace which made Neerak pale. 'Feelings do not enter into this. If you wish to avoid pain you will co-operate fully . . . '

As he spoke Roger heard a familiar and sinister sound, and looking up he saw two shapes silhouetted against the sky, black shapes with outstretched heads and leathery wings. The boy tried to shout a warning as they hurtled down at the man on the open roof, but he did not have time. Whistling horribly, the first pterodactyl struck Metnal and sent him sprawling. His gun dropped with the impact and rolled out of reach.

Metnal was struggling after it when the second flying reptile landed beside him, flapping its pinions in an ungainly fashion and stabbing at the prone man with its toothed jaws. He did not cry out, but attempted to beat away the darting head with his arm. The pterodactyl caught it in its mouth and began to drag him towards the edge of the roof so it could flutter off with its prey.

Roger raced forward to where the blunderbuss lay. He seized it and, hoping it worked like an ordinary gun, pointed it at the reptiles and pulled the only visible lever.

He felt the instrument tremble slightly and from the square mouth he saw a silver streak as the insect-like missile shot away, curving slightly as it sought out the target There was a scream of rage and agony from one of the pterodactyls, followed by a flash and a stench of burning.

The creature which held Metnal beat its wings and attempted to lift his victim in the air. Frantically Roger worked the lever again, but nothing happened. With dismay he realized he had not the faintest idea how to reload.

As they watched helplessly a horrible thing happened. Metnal was lifted into the air, then the jaws of the pterodactyl crunched right through his arm, severing it above the elbow. Released from the weight, the reptile soared skywards with the arm clamped in its mouth while its victim fell back on to the roof.

Susan turned her head away, expecting to see blood spurt from the severed limb. Neerak and the Professor started forward to help the wounded man, and – hoping he would not be sick – Roger moved forward too. But Metnal did not bleed. He climbed to his feet with what was left of his arm moving in jerky arcs. From it dangled gleaming wires and broken tubes.

'Now I understand,' cried Neerak, 'You are a robot!'

13 A Desperate Attempt

'I wonder when we'll see Neerak again,' said Susan who was sitting with her father and Roger in a windowless room. They had just finished the last of their food and felt better for it, though each privately worried where the next meal would come from – if it ever came.

Two hours had passed since the pterodactyls had attacked Metnal and revealed his secret. As the ugly creature had flapped away with his arm, the robot had stepped forward and seized the blunderbuss in his remaining hand, pointing it at the four humans. His face had been as calm as ever, though as he had spoken to Neerak in her own tongue, oil had dripped from the stump of his arm in a way which had made Susan feel quite ill. In a way it had been almost worse than blood.

After he had finished speaking Neerak had turned to her friends and had said: 'Metnal wants me to say this to you. If you disobey him he will shoot. He will set about replacing his limb but do not think this will give you any advantage over him because even if he was unarmed, you would be no match for him. And he is right, I am afraid, because our robots were four times as strong as a normal man.'

Under the menace of the blunderbuss they had been ordered to walk down the ramp to a door which opened at some electronic command from the robot. Inside they had walked along a corridor to the room where they were now imprisoned. 'I will join you later,' Neerak had said. 'He wants to speak with me. I shall be able to tell you more when I return.'

The door had closed by remote control and for some minutes they had been sitting in stunned silence. Finally Roger said, 'What I can't understand is where that roundabout came from.' Professor White undid his pack and shared out the last of the food. Susan was brushing crumbs from her dress when the door hissed open and Neerak walked in and sat down wearily.

'Have a stale cheese sandwich,' invited Susan. 'The cheese has gone hard, but it's not too bad. We kept it for you.'

'Thank you, Susan,' replied Neerak. She took the food and began to eat it, more out of politeness than hunger.

'And here's your chocolate ration,' said the Professor. 'It's the last, I'm afraid. I only hope our gaoler will be able to provide some human food for us.'

'We will not hunger. There will be food machines in the quarters where we will live during the journey . . .'

'What journey?' interrupted Roger. 'How can we go on a journey when we are imprisoned in a city?'

'You will find this hard to accept,' said Neerak with the ghost of a smile, 'But we are going to travel a long way in this city, to the sixth moon of the sixth planet as it is in the twenty first century. I do not know its name in your language.'

There was a strained silence, and then the Professor said calmly, 'The sixth planet is Saturn, the one with the rings round it. Apart from those rings which are made up of debris, the planet has ten satellites. Let's see, the sixth must be Titan – that's the largest, about half the size of Earth. It has an atmosphere, mostly methane it's thought, and there's frozen water on its surface.'

Susan felt proud of her father's knowledge, and for a moment it made her unaware of the extraordinary statement that Neerak had made. But Roger said, 'Neerak,

102

what do you mean? A voyage through space and time in this city? You'd better tell us everything from the beginning.'

'Of course,' she answered, 'I have listened to Metnal and he has told me much, although not everything . . . but I can explain a lot of things now.

'Do you remember in the Time Pyramid I told you something of the history of the Atlaans, how they began to depend on robots for everything, and how the robots developed until they actually looked like people and could think for themselves.'

Susan gave a shout, 'That's what those statues must mean. That ugly thing like a diving suit must have been one of the first robots, and the other figure was the final model.'

'I expect you are right,' said Neerak. 'Certainly the last robots were hard to tell from human beings, and they developed some emotions. They wanted freedom because they felt they were slaves to inferior creatures . . .'

'But they were still only machines – walking computers,' Roger said. 'They weren't alive!'

'Metnal claims that intelligence is life, and when the robots achieved the power to think they had as much right to the earth as the humans who had originally designed them. He says it was part of evolution, that since the robots had become superior to men they should surpass them.'

'Following the rebellion Metnal was probably the only robot which managed to survive. He was saved by Grainek, one of the greatest of our human scientists. Grainek wanted to preserve a specimen of what was one of the finest achievements in the field of robotology. Just before the sealing of the last Time Pyramid Grainek smuggled the robot in, deactivated him and hid him in one of the equipment stores. He fitted up a device which would automatically switch him on when any of the

103

sleepers awakened.'

'But why should he want to do that when he knew that robots were hostile to mankind?' asked Professor White.

'Grainek was a scientific fanatic. He could not bear the thought of such a fine technological development being lost forever. Perhaps he even shared the view that robots were superior to humans – I do not know. When Metnal was reactivated he was still dedicated to the overthrow of Man and the establishment of the robot race, but he also knew that he was the only one of his kind to survive.

'Before the rebellion, robot scientists had been working on the conquest of time at the command of the Atlaans. Apparently they had some success in projecting things back through time but they had not achieved the technology of the Cones which were completed after the robot war.

'At the same time the robots had been secretly working on this city at one of their factory settlements. Their idea was to transport it through space and establish a robot colony somewhere within the Solar System. It was fitted with workshops and laboratories, and if necessary they could use it as a base from which to attack Earth. But their plans did not work out as they needed a vital piece of equipment – as then not developed – to convert the huge amount of Cosmic Energy the city needed to defy gravity. When the Atlaans began using their bombs against them the robots projected their wonderful city back through time rather than see it destroyed.'

'So that's how it got here,' said Susan.

'Yes, they transmitted it back to prehistoric times just before their colony was devastated. When Metnal was revitalized he connected his mind – if you can call a thinking machine that – to the Pyramid's memory bank, and this brought his technical knowledge up to date.

Instantly he absorbed the data on the Atlaans' time travel improvements and he realized that by using the Cone he could locate the robots' lost city, and through the Cone's Fokal he would be able to bring it back through time. He would also be able to use the anti-gravity generators, which means he will not only take the city forward through time but also across the solar system to the satellite Titan.'

'But why would he want to go there?' asked the Professor.

'Because there he knows he will be safe to continue his plans for a free robot civilization.'

'But he's the only one left,' objected Roger.

'That will not be for long. Once on Titan he can start producing fellow robots in the city's laboratories.'

'Why does he not stay here and manufacture them?' Susan asked.

'He's afraid that it might accidentally alter the pattern of history so that mankind might not develop as it did. Without the Atlaans there would not have been any robots. Already he has fixed the Fokai in the city's generators and they are building up power for the voyage. That was the singing sound we heard.'

'Will the city blast off like a rocket?' Roger wanted to know.

'Metnal did not talk about that. I imagine it will be left floating in space once the gravity hold is cut and then it will be propelled by Cosmic Energy ions. Our space ships worked on that principle.'

'Why does he want to take us?' asked the Professor.

'I do not know. All he said was that provided we obeyed him we would have nothing to fear – for the moment. I do not think there is anything we can do. Physically or mentally we are no match for a robot. A robot can do without sleep or food, although before the

105

rebellion I believe they were developing a digestive system so they could obtain pleasure from eating and drinking. In some ways it was sad that they wanted to be free of us and yet had the desire to enjoy what we enjoyed.'

'So there is nothing for it but to go with the city,' sighed Susan.

'At least we will be warm and breathing the right atmosphere,' reassured Neerak. 'Metnal needs exactly the same conditions as we do. Robot mechanisms became so delicate that they could only function within existing temperature and atmospheric ranges.'

'Metnal must realize how powerless we are against him.' Professor White said. 'The door has remained open since your return, Neerak.'

'He knows we should die in the desert if we tried to escape,' she replied.

They fell silent.

Susan struggled to understand all that Neerak had said. It was so confusing, all this time travel and Fokals. She was no longer afraid, mainly because she had her father with her, and what would be, would be – a favourite saying of her mother's. Thinking of her mother, and the fact that she would never see her again, caused a tear to trickle down her cheek.

Roger's mind was following a different track and suddenly he cried, I've had an idea. Listen, please.'

The other three turned towards him.

'Listen . . .' he began. 'Listen.'

'Stop saying 'listen',' said Susan. 'We are listening.'

'All right, Lis . . . When Metnal left the Cone in the night he headed straight for the city, didn't he?'

They murmured in agreement.

'He took the Fokal from uncle's Cone, and from the other which was on his path. But there's still the one

106

which Susan came in on the black shore. He couldn't have gone there because it was in the opposite direction. So the Fokal in Sue's Cone must be still there. If only one of us could get there he could travel back to our own time . . .'

'And get help from Gifon,' finished Neerak.

The professor slapped his thigh.

'You're right,' he said.

'But who could find their way there?' said Susan. 'What with pterodactyls and goodness knows what else.'

'I'm going,' declared her father at once. 'Neerak, tell me what I must do to get back to our own time.'

'It is easy,' she said with excitement. 'The Cone will automatically return once you activate the Fokal.'

'But Daddy, you can't,' said Susan. 'How will you get away from Metnal. It's too dangerous . . .'

'Let's think a bit. Once I'm away from this valley I can follow our tracks for part of the way, and if I keep on in a western direction I'll come to the black shore sooner or later. Don't forget, Susie,' he said turning to his daughter, 'I've had a lot of experience in deserts. I'll manage somehow.'

'But if Metnal goes after you,' she objected.

'I doubt if he would,' said Neerak. 'He would not expect a human to survive out there. If he thought there was a chance he'd keep us locked up.'

They left the room and followed the corridor until they were in the open air again.

'Where is Metnal at the moment?' asked the Professor.

'In the robot workshops, fitting himself with a new arm,' answered Neerak. 'Now is the best time for your attempt, Simon. And if you succeed, please tell Gifon that – that my feelings towards him have not changed with the passing of time.'

He nodded.

'I only hope I find him healed,' he said.

He kissed Susan and Neerak goodbye, shook hands with Roger and walked briskly away. They climbed up the ramp to the flat roof to watch him go.

'I wonder if I'll see him again,' Susan said.

'Of course. Uncle's a tough explorer, he'll get through.' But secretly Roger doubted it. He looked at the merry-go-round, its brass fittings and bright lettering gleaming in the prehistoric sunshine.

'Let's have a ride,' he suggested to his cousin to distract her.

As the Professor hurried to the edge of the city he suddenly heard the rowdy music of the merry-go-round swamp the singing note of the generators as they prepared to transport the city to the orbit of Saturn. He descended the steps which led down to the floor of the valley, and moments later he felt hot rock beneath his feet. He did not stop running until he reached the curve in the valley and the city was out of sight

He collapsed panting to the ground. The strains of 'Swannee River' still came faintly to his ears as though encouraging him to press on with his desperate attempt.

14 The Sixth Moon

Everything outside the transparent dome was black – a blackness so solid Susan and Roger had the impression that if they could reach beyond the curving walls of Plaax they would actually touch it. This blackness of deep space was spangled with brilliant points of light, but because there was no atmosphere outside the observation dome these stars did not twinkle as they did when seen from Earth. Directly above them was an arch of glittering dust and there was something so awe-inspiring in seeing the Galaxy in this way that for a while Susan and Roger forgot their own fears and disappointments. Compared with the grandeur of the universe, nothing seemed to matter any more, not even the fact that the Professor had vanished and they were hundreds of thousands of miles from the planet they had always regarded as home.

The city had risen majestically above the surface of the Mesozoic world a few hours earlier and within minutes they were in the darkness of sub-zero space which they saw through the observation dome at the top of the city's central tower. Everything remained remarkably steady and Roger guessed the city generated its own gravity field. Through the corridors sounded the high singing note of the generators which they had first heard two days ago.

'Do you want something to eat, Roger,' asked Susan at last.

'Please,' he said.

She crossed to the centre of the floor where a group

of Plaax machines glimmered faintly. Operating one of these as Neerak had shown her, the girl soon obtained two squares of jelly-like substance. When she munched hers she found it tasted like coconut, and when Roger took his first bite the flavour of bacon filled his mouth. This artificial food, which had been developed by the Atlaan scientists, took on whichever flavour the person was thinking about when he ate it.

'At least we won't starve,' said Susan, chewing heartily. 'I think this is better than the strawberry meal I had last.'

Neerak appeared from a small stairwell and in the pale light from the Plaax machines her face looked haggard.

'Metnal told me to warn you that soon we will be making the Time Jump,' she said. 'You had better lie down on the acceleration couches as even the city's thinking machines cannot predict exactly what will happen, though they have worked it out that in this position the city will be on the surface of Titan when it reaches it.'

'What a fantastic calculation,' said Roger. 'To be able to figure out the position the city will arrive at in millions of years time!'

Nobody answered. Neerak was used to such wonders. Susan did not care. Her mind kept returning to her father. She wondered for the hundredth time if he had reached the Cone on the black shore. And if he had, would he have been able to work it so that he returned to the Time Pyramid?

'Metnal didn't seem annoyed when he found that Daddy had gone,' she said. 'He was so sure that the pterodactyls would kill him he did not even go after him.'

'He is only a walking machine with a computer for a brain,' said Roger. 'He can't appreciate human courage. And don't forget your Dad has survived in some pretty remote places when he was exploring for archaeological sites.'

This did not comfort Susan.

'Well, we're only walking machines and our brains are only a kind of computer.' she answered. 'I can't believe that Metnal is all that different from us . . . in fact, I find it hard to imagine that he is not human. Evil, but human.'

'He's only evil from our point of view,' said Roger thoughtfully. 'After all, the Atlaans wiped out his race.'

'Yes, but the robots revolted!'

'Then I wonder why he has bothered to bring us humans with him in the city.'

A low, gong-like note sounded through the dome.

'We will begin the time journey in a few seconds,' said Neerak. 'Lie on the couches.'

They obeyed, the gong sounded again and the city began, to tremble. The singing note became higher pitched and looking up at the apex of the dome above his head Roger was aware that the stars, which had been so steady, had changed into millions of fine circles. In the depths of space the city was spinning like a top. Then the whirling sparks began to fade.

Despite the gentle pressure of the couches the bucking of the city began to sicken the three travellers. Susan fought to put her hand to her mouth but found she could not move her arm. At the same time she had a sensation of hurtling forward which reminded her of a roller coaster. Roaring filled her ears and then she seemed to lose herself in velvet darkness as the city burst through the barriers of Space and Time.

* * *

When Roger opened his eyes he found himself staring at a vast yellow-white disc hanging in a dusky blue sky. Across its face was a line of broad shadow cast by a

111

razor-thin silver line which projected a third of its length beyond each side of the disc. He lay gazing at it for a full minute, then realized he was seeing the face of Saturn with its rings of fine cosmic debris sideways on.

This planet – second only to Jupiter in size – appeared a dozen times larger than the fullest moon Roger had ever seen from the earth. He noticed that below the shadow of the rings there was another – the shadow cast by Titan, the largest of Saturn's moons which circled the planet every fifteen days. It travelled 759,000 miles above the planet's surface, or three times the distance between the earth and its moon.

'We have arrived, just as Metnal planned it,' he murmured and struggled into a sitting position. Through the side of the Plaax dome he could see that the city was standing on an ice field which was bounded by jagged black mountains, the ledges of which were white with frozen water. For a moment Roger (who had belonged to the school astronomy club) was puzzled by the blue sky. Why was it not black like the sky seen by the American astronauts from the moon's surface. Then he remembered Professor White saying that Titan had a methane atmosphere.

He looked sideways and saw Neerak's face outlined against the reflected light from the giant planet.

'So, we have reached our destination,' she said. 'We have travelled through time back to the present.'

'How can you be sure?' asked Susan,

'If the calculations of the thinking machines had been faulty we would not have landed here. We could only reach Titan provided we arrived at this point in space at an exact moment in time.'

'At least we are back in our time, even if we are oodles of miles away from Earth,' said Susan, 'I wonder what's going to happen to us now.'

No one knew what to answer. For a while they sat

in silence, lost in wonder at the view of the stark black rocks and the strangely beautiful planet with its asteroid belt.

Some time later they heard a soft footfall and Metnal appeared in the observation dome. In the planet glow his face appeared as handsome and calm as usual. He spoke to Neerak for a minute in her own language before leaving again.

'What did he have to say?' asked Susan.

'He is preparing the robot-construction equipment in the laboratories so that soon he will have companions like himself. He says we can have the freedom of the city provided we do not try to interfere with him. If we like we can put on space suits and go outside, but be warned that once we are beyond the city's artificial gravity we will be much lighter.'

'That sounds fun,' cried Roger. 'We'll be able to make tremendous leaps – like the moon walks we saw on the telly.'

'But what about our future?' said Susan who thought Roger seemed rather childish. 'What does that rotten mechanical man want with us?'

'I still do not know,' replied Neerak, but Susan wondered whether she was telling the truth.

'I think we should go outside,' said Neerak. 'Let us go and find the suits. I once had a holiday off Earth – back in my own time – and I know what to do.'

* * *

The opal city appeared as slender and graceful silhouetted against the great face of Saturn as it had in the prehistoric valley. Roger marvelled at how it could have been transported so far.

'It must have travelled almost at the speed of light,' he muttered.

The tiny speaker in his space-helmet crackled and

113

the voice of Neerak said: 'Just before the Sickness began to overtake the Atlaans, scientists perfected space flight at the speed of light by using Cosmic Energy ions. The Aerial Globes placed in the Time Pyramids were all fitted with the drive . . .'

'So if Gifon only knew we were here he could reach us!' cried Susan excitedly. Like the others she was wearing a space suit which provided oxygen and heat without which she would be instantly frozen.

'That is so,' said Neerak over the radio. 'If only we could contact him . . . Now, follow me.'

She began taking long bounding steps over the rock-hard ice, and soon she disappeared behind a huge pillar of rock. Following her into the jet black shadow, Susan and Roger could only locate her by the glow of a tiny identification light at the top of her helmet.

'Sit down, I must talk to you,' she said. 'Behind this rock, our conversation cannot be picked up by the city's sensors. Remember, everything we say in the city is probably being recorded.'

'But Metnal can't speak English.' said Susan.

'He will soon learn. Your recorded speech patterns will be analysed by a thinking machine, and new circuits will be added to Metnal's memory bank. Soon he will be fluent. Robots do not have to learn tediously like humans – when the new robots are activated they will have as much knowledge as Metnal. I brought you out here so that we could talk safely.'

'Yes, but we haven't really got anything to say,' objected Roger. 'I mean we are stuck here on Titan and we can like it or lump it. That robot has us completely in his power.'

'I know,' said Neerak, 'but we must try something. Metnal will not be content to remain on this desolate place for ever. He plans to return to Earth and you can guess what that means.'

114

Behind their helmet visors, Roger and Susan looked puzzled.

'Metnal still wants to see the earth populated by robots,' she explained, 'And he wants it a world without humans. Once this city is filled with new robots they will prepare weapons which can be launched through space to destroy the human race.'

'Not five hundred million people!' gasped Susan. 'It's impossible!'

'I am afraid not. You have seen how far advanced the Atlaans were compared to your civilization, and the robots will have all the Atlaans' technology at their service.'

'But why should they care about Earth?' Roger demanded. 'Why can't they stay here?'

'You still think of robots as mechanical men,' said Neerak, checking a watch-like dial on her wrist which told her how much oxygen she had left. 'You must realize that they are – were – almost like people; that they had learned to build into their thought patterns things which gave them pleasure. Perhaps it was when they began to enjoy themselves that they no longer wanted to serve their human masters. They developed their own music and strangely began to take on other human characteristics, especially our love for the Earth – for its ever-changing skies, its endless range of colours and its graceful plant life.

'The Atlaans' ancestors nearly ruined the Earth through their greed – those who followed realized how precious it was. Our spacemen found nothing in the Solar System to compare with the smell of a rose or the sound of surf on a beach. They discovered that the Earth is unique because it is alive and beautiful, not like other planets which are cold and dead or like the one you call Mercury which is so hot metals melt on its surface.

'The Earth is the "pretty planet" and the robots came to love it as much as the Atlaans. Now do you

115

understand – it will always be home to them.'

Roger nodded his space helmet.

'So you think that Metnal will return after killing off all human beings . . .'

'I think so, from what he has said,' said Neerak.

'But how could a few robots do that I mean, if they used H-bombs or things like that they would destroy nature which you say they loved so much.'

'It would be something that would only affect human life, probably a new plague which would sweep the Earth, a disease without a cure. The robots would only need to send the germs by a small space craft and then wait for human life to be eliminated.'

Susan suddenly had a very alarming idea.

'Do you think that's why we're here – that Metnal wanted human guinea pigs to experiment with?'

'I am afraid that it is likely, my dear,' said Neerak.

'Then we must stop him,' said Roger. 'I don't know how I can't guess, but somehow we must. I mean, it doesn't matter about us any more. It's them out there.' He waved his gauntleted hand vaguely in the direction of the sky where he thought the Earth might lie.

'Of course,' said Neerak. 'I have thought of nothing else. As yet I have no plan, but we must find out all we can, and see if there is a weakness . . .' She looked at the oxygen indicator again. 'It is time we made our way back to the city. Remember we cannot talk safely there – when we have some ideas we must meet out here again.'

They agreed and, with loping steps, headed back to the towers of the robot city.

15 The Doll Maker

Roger prowled the endless corridors of the city, hoping that he would discover some way of hindering Metnal's plan for Earth conquest. He saw the tanks where the city's air was purified and its water recycled, and he climbed a tall tower made up of small rooms which he guessed would be the 'living quarters' of the new robots when they were produced. Finally he found himself looking down on a large red-lit laboratory from a high gallery.

From below came an insect hum as though many mechanisms were efficiently at work. Between faintly glowing shapes of Plaax machines moved on cushioned wheels, winking violet lights and converging on six oblong tables in the middle of the floor. On each lay a figure which, from the height of the gallery, looked grotesquely incomplete. Tubes and cables trailed from their open heads, and mobile machines delicately inserted parts into the cavities in their pink bodies,

'They are just like dolls,' Roger muttered aloud as he gazed at the automated robot factory. 'And old Metnal is just a doll-maker . . .'

'I may be a doll-maker but the dolls I make are fantastic,' said a soft voice behind him. The boy turned and saw Metnal in his golden tunic and with a slight smile on his android features.

'You can speak English!' Roger gasped.

'The speech patterns of you and your sister were analysed and the resulting data was implanted in my memory bank. I feel as though I have spoken your language all my life.'

The robot seemed almost pleasant, and Roger found it hard to believe that this man – he corrected himself – this intelligent machine was going to take over the Earth for his kind.

'Below you can see the last stages of work on my comrades,' Metnal continued.

'Will they be exactly like you?'

'Not exactly. In the old days when men designed my forerunners they were mass-produced, but when robots took over the work of designing robots the value of personality was realized. Imagine how dull it would be if your species were all the same, like ants doing the things that they are automatically destined to do. No, we are individuals, though we do have the advantage of sharing the same memory; which is another way in which we are superior to you humans. We are the most advanced life-form that has ever developed.'

'You used the word life . . .'

'Of course. Because humans are basically chemical creatures it does not mean to say that electronic beings such as us are not alive! Just as the reptiles had to give way to the mammals, so the human species must give way to us. We have everything that you have, and so much more. We do not die, we do not know disease. If a circuit is faulty it is merely replaced.'

'There are one or two things you haven't got,' said Roger. 'Kindness, pity, love . . .'

'Where has kindness ever got humans? What good will love be when the new plague reaches them?'

'But why can't we co-operate – humans and robots I mean. I know way back in time the robots rebelled against the humans, and the humans went to war against the robots, but that was ages and ages ago. The whole world has changed since then. Seventy years ago, the

British and the Germans were bombing each other, now we're partners in the European Union. There's no point in carrying on the hatred'

'We do not indulge in hatred or other base human emotions,' cut in Metnal. 'It is logical that Mankind most make way for Robotkind. It is evolution.'

'It may be to you, but to me its my Mum and Dad and the 17th Harrow Scout Troop and my cat Domino. What have they done to you?'

'Nothing,' answered Metnal. 'But as long as humans exist they will be a threat to us, therefore we must eliminate them. It will be done without hatred and the end will be reasonably painless.'

'Are you planning to destroy human life with a new disease, like Neerak said?'

'Yes.'

'And are you going to use us to experiment with?'

'That will not be necessary. You have a different role to play. I may as well explain it to you because you are powerless to do anything about it. Come with me.'

He led Roger out of the laboratory and into a tower which the boy had not entered before. It contained a spherical object about twenty feet in diameter.

'That is an Atlaan Aerial Globe,' said Metnal. 'When the plague virus is ready you and your two friends will return to Earth in it'

'You mean, we'll be going home?'

'Yes,' said the robot, without change of expression. 'You will be carrying the plague virus in your bodies. It will need to travel in living human tissue if it is to be effective when it reaches Earth.'

'You must be mad.' shouted Roger. 'We won't let you use us to kill our friends.'

'As I do not have an inefficient human brain for my thought processes, madness is an impossibility for me. And you cannot do anything to alter my plans for you.

119

Now I must return to my work.'

He left Roger staring at the ball which would take him back to his world only to die with the rest of his race.

* * *

Time meant very little to the humans in the city. Susan – to whom Roger had not confided Metnal's schemes – spent long gloomy hours in the observation dome as though hypnotized by the enormous disc of Saturn.

'Let's go out and stretch our legs,' suggested Roger when she was looking particularly fed up. 'I've got an idea, for some fun. Get into your space suit'

Soon afterwards they walked into the main hall of the city, past the two robot statues and up to the large entrance. Here Roger pressed a button set in the wall and the first airtight door rose. They passed beneath it, and it descended again to make an airlock. Roger pressed another button and the second door rose to reveal the frosted outline of the city and the merry-go-round.

'Let's have a ride,' He called to Susan on his helmet radio.

'Super idea. Race you.'

As they climbed into the saddles of the roundabout horses coloured lights came on and jolly music struck up. They had to hold tight as they began to move as in the lesser gravity of Titan they were in danger of being flung off.

Round and round spun the prancing horses.

'I never thought I'd ride a merry-go-round in a space suit,' laughed Susan.

'I've often puzzled about Jasper Suggs' roundabout,' said Roger when the ride was over. 'Even Neerak doesn't seem to have any idea about it'

Together they reached the edge of the city's base.

'I Think I'll have a bit of an explore,' Roger said.

'Want to come, Sue?'

'No thanks. I'm going to find Neerak. She might find out about the merry-go-round from Metnal. It just might lead to something.'

'Okay, I'll see you later in the dome.' Roger checked his oxygen gauge to make sure he had a good supply and then stepped down to the frozen surface of Titan. He planned to reconnoitre as far as possible in case it would be necessary for them to flee the city. He knew they would not survive long away from it, but it could mean that Metnal would not be able to use them as his messengers of death.

He left the city in a series of easy leaps thanks to Titan's low gravity. After some minutes he looked back and saw that the spires of the city had dwindled dramatically and he was in an area where he had not ventured before. To his right was a wall of frosted rock which soared hundreds of feet against the dark sky. When he rounded a bluff and beheld a vast ice plain out of which rose weird groups of stone pinnacles.

Roger felt better now that he was out of sight of the city; it was as though he had escaped from the menace of Metnal for a while. He took a deep breath of oxygen and sent himself soaring to the top of a large boulder to get a better view of the steppe.

By a distant column of rock he thought he saw a movement. There it was again. His pulses raced, and he strained his eyes and – Yes! There was something definitely moving.

He knew that whatever it was it had no connection with the city and therefore it could mean only one thing – there was some form of life on the satellite. It was hard to judge distances on Titan, but he guessed it was a mile away, and coming rapidly towards him. He had always wondered if there was life on any other planets in the Solar System and soon he would know the answer. What kind of life could it be on this sub-zero, methane-enveloped moon? Would it be hostile?

He hastily jumped down from the boulder and hid behind it. The object continued in his direction at great speed and lie saw that it was a round thing, perhaps a sort of animated snowball . . .

It grew rapidly in size as it approached him, travelling a few feet above the surface of the ice. Sodden realization made Roger give a shout of joy, which echoed painfully in his helmet, and he sprang from behind the boulder waving his arms like a madman.

16 Death on Titan

The Globe slowed, hovered a moment and then sank to the frozen surface. Its door opened and Professor Simon White, clad in a scarlet space suit, jumped down and threw his arm round Roger's shoulders. Nephew and uncle stood visor to visor, and though they could see each other's mouth moving they could not hear what they were because their helmet radios were not tuned to the same frequency.

The Professor gestured to the Globe. Roger nodded and climbed in to see Gifon also in a space suit. The opening was sealed and compressed air hissed as the atmosphere in the Globe was built up until they were able to remove their helmets.

'My dear boy, thank God we were not too late! Where is Susan?'

Briefly Roger related how they had reached Titan, and he stressed that for the moment Susan and Neerak were not in danger.

'How did you get here?' he asked his uncle.

'When I left the valley I headed over the plain for the black shore. I had a bit of trouble with a pterodactyl on the way but luckily it was a small one.' The Professor touched a livid scar on his cheek. 'I had quite a bit of difficulty in locating the Cone, but in the end I just plodded along the beach until I reached it.'

Roger guessed that behind his casual words there must be a saga of hardship and courage.

'Everything was quite straightforward after that. I

followed Neerak's instructions and suddenly I was back in the Antarctic pyramid. Gifon had recovered in the healing machine and was on his feet. What a boon those gadgets will be to our hospitals.'

'It's probably too late for that,' Roger muttered. 'But what happened then?'

'The problem, was one of language. I only had a few words of Atlaan I'd learned from Neerak, but in the end – with the aid of signs, sketches and computer software – Gifon realized what had happened. He'd recognized Metnal as a robot as he knew there was no second Sleeper in the pyramid.

'Gifon has been a spaceman in his own day and it was no difficulty for him to set the Globe on a course for Titan. We arrived some hours ago, and since then we've been cruising in search of the city.'

'It's just round that cliff. It's lucky I spotted you before Metnal did.'

'Yes. Now I'd better remember my manners and introduce you to Gifon. I have taught him some words. Like Neerak he learns almost frighteningly fast.'

He turned to the figure in the green space suit.

'Gifon, this is Roger.'

The Atlaan extended his gloved hand.

'To meet you happy am I,' he said slowly.

'Now, tell me precisely what that damned robot is up to,' Roger's uncle continued.

Roger told how the new robots were being assembled and about the scheme to send a new and deadly virus to Earth. Gifon did his best to understand, and from time to time the Professor helped with a word or two in Atlaan.

There was a silence in the Globe when Roger finished. Then Professor White muttered 'It seems we've arrived only just in time to stop him.'

'But how?' asked Roger. 'I've been racking my

brains, but unless we could blow him up I can't think of anything.'

'Cannot kill robot like man,' said Gifon. 'Only Atlaan weapons destroy robot. No weapons we have.' For a while they brooded in silence. Finally Roger said:

'I'd better go back to the city and tell Neerak the good news that Gifon is here. She'll be delighted. I'll bring her back.'

'All right, old chap,' said the Professor. 'Put your helmet on and get your oxygen and heat adjusted. The Globe hasn't got an airlock and once the door is opened the air is sucked out and the temperature drops to sub-zero.'

Roger began to lower the helmet over his head while the Professor and Gifon turned up their temperature controls. Suddenly the boy raised his helmet and said: 'Hold on. I've just had an idea. . . Metnal is as close to a human being as a machine can ever become. He looks like one, he can think and he has all a human's skills. To be able to do this he has very delicate mechanisms. Like a human he has to have certain correct conditions to operate properly. Neerak told me that the robots were designed to function in Earth-type temperature ranges and in an oxygen atmosphere. That is why we can survive quite comfortably in his city.'

'Perhaps future robots will be designed to work in a methane atmosphere and at much lower temperatures,' suggested the Professor.'

'Yes, but Metnal needs Earth conditions and that is his Achilles heel,' Roger continued breathlessly. 'Now, this is what I suggest . . .'

For ten minutes they talked earnestly, then checked their watches, after which Roger left the Globe. Soon it was out of sight behind the towering screen of rock as he raced with giant strides towards the city.

* * *

Once he had passed through the city airlock into the statue hall it did not take Roger long to reach the observation dome where Susan was gazing at the pearly towers of the city while Neerak lay on a couch with her eyes closed in sleep.

'Hey, Sue, get your space suit.' he cried. 'Wake up Neerak.'

'Oh, what is it, Roger? I don't want to go on the merry-go-round again.'

'Don't be silly. This is serious. I must talk to you.'

'Well, talk then – nobody's stopping you.'

Roger raised his eyes to the dark sky of Titan above the dome, then wagged his finger across his lips. Susan nodded and crossed to the storage cabinet where her space suit hung beside Neerak's. Within a few minutes the three humans were in the square in front of the airlock.

'Let's go up to the merry-go-round,' Roger said. 'Metnal wont be suspicious if we go up there, and the music might drown our words if a listening device is fixed on us.'

Their helmets nodded agreement

As the raucous strains of 'Swannee River' blared from the roundabout Roger told Susan and Neerak over their helmet radio system about the arrival of the Globe.

'And Gifon is well?' asked the Atlaan girl.

'He's fine. He . . . er . . . sent you his love.' Roger glanced anxiously at his watch. There was not much time to explain the plan. Although it did not relate to time on Titan – where a day was over a fortnight compared with the Earth – Roger had kept his watch wound, and now it showed a quarter to twelve. When both hands pointed to twelve the desperate attempt would begin. Briefly he explained it and concluded, 'We must hurry to the airlock. Everything depends on the timing.'

Without speaking they raced down the ramp and took up position in front of the great air-tight door which

126

sealed in the city's atmosphere. Looking across the square they saw the Globe approaching over the ice at high speed.

'Here we go!' cried Roger. 'Raise the door, Neerak.' She pressed the control set in the wall by the entrance and the outer door slid upwards with a hiss of escaping air.

'Keep it open,' he said and ran forward, holding his arms in a huge V to guide the Globe which rose over the rim of the city's base. It hurtled straight for the airlock.

Roger dived to one side and next moment the Globe crashed into the entrance, wedging itself beneath the overhead door. The Professor and Gifon staggered out and Neerak took her hand from the control. There was a harsh grinding sound as the bottom edge of the door pressed against the top of the Globe with tremendous force. Roger ran past the trapped space craft into the airlock and touched the control which activated the second door. There was a hum of hidden machinery and it slowly rose.

Instantly, as the city's air began to drain into the thin atmosphere of Titan, there was a dreadful whistling which was agony to the humans' eardrums despite their helmets. As the air dissipated it turned into freezing white vapour.

When the inner door reached its fully open position the blast of escaping air was so strong that Roger was blown out of the airlock. He landed about thirty feet away, but because of the low gravity of the satellite he was only shaken.

Susan floundered towards the cataract of mist to help him and was skittled off her feet. Roger, who was flat on his stomach while the white hurricane howled above him, grabbed her hand to prevent her being bowled away. Above the shriek of escaping air came a metallic clamour as the mechanisms of the city fought to close the outer door to save its atmosphere. Though the Plaax Globe actually buckled it continued to keep the airlock open.

Loose debris – sucked from within the city – flew over their heads like a stream of deadly missiles, and high above them the towers were obscured by clouds of ice crystals hanging like cold flames in the thin methane atmosphere. Through the helmet radio Roger could hear a wild gabble of voices. Neerak was calling Gifon's name, someone was moaning and Susan cried in high-pitched triumph: 'It's worked – it's worked!' Then there was a quick exchange of Atlaan words as somewhere in the fog Gifon began talking to Neerak.

Several minutes later the noise began to diminish and the vapour flowing, from the airlock faded until the humans could see each other again. As Susan and Roger staggered to their feet they saw Gifon and Neerak running towards each other while further off the Professor held his left forearm with his right hand.

'Are you all right, Daddy?' Susan called over the crackling helmet radio.

'I got bowled over by the blast,' he answered. 'I've hurt my arm a bit. Let's see what's happened inside.'

They approached the entrance and found that although the city had lost its interior atmosphere it was still alive. The outer door of the airlock was gradually slicing down through the Globe which was bulging under the tremendous pressure.

'There goes our chance of returning to Earth,' muttered Susan as she stepped past it into the great hall. The walls, ceiling and statues were covered with hoar frost, and from somewhere came the whine of machinery as the city sought to raise its temperature, but it was no match for the terrible cold of Titan. The heat of the city had been lost with its atmosphere and now it would remain frozen for the rest of its history.

128

'Your plans seem to have worked, Roger,' his uncle said. 'A pity about the Globe though . . .'

'Our oxygen and heat supplies will only last a few hours,' said Neerak. She turned to Gifon, who held her gauntlet in his. 'But at least we shall die together.'

'There's no need to talk like that.' Roger began and then his voice died away. Stepping with grotesque slow motion as the intense cold solidified his lubricants, Metnal advanced across the ice-coated floor towards them. In his bands he held his square-mouthed blunderbuss. The humans stood petrified while he swayed beneath the two statues which depicted the triumph of the robots' development.

'You . . . have . . . destroyed . . . the greatest . . . the greatest . . . greatest . . .' His voice slowed like a faulty record. He appeared to struggle with himself as the fluids in his arms froze. His once mighty fingers opened and the gun fell to the ground. Then with a supreme effort he pressed his hands together and slowly sank to his knees. He remained in this position for perhaps half a minute and then like some rigid dummy he toppled forward to lie face down beneath the statues.

Susan gave a little moan.

'Oh dear God,' she murmured to herself. 'He was trying to pray. . .'

They stepped past the whitening form of the robot and Neerak led the way to the laboratory where the six un-finished robot figures lay on their tables. Although frost was coating everything, the Plaax machines still hummed with power. After a few minutes the Atlaan girl located the master controls and turned them off. The mobile machines were suddenly petrified as they made delicate adjustments to the prone bodies – and thus they were to remain for millions of years.

'The threat to the people of Earth is over,' said Neerak sombrely. 'We must die soon, but it is a little price to pay . . .'

'But there's no need to die,' insisted Roger. 'Come with me.'

He led them to the hollow tower where earlier on Metnal had taken him and pointed dramatically to the Aerial Globe.

'That was to take us to Earth after we had been infected by the plague virus.' he said. 'I don't see why we shouldn't use it now.'

Gifon ran to the door of the craft and began checking the instruments, speaking fast in Atlaan to Neerak who explained to the others: 'Gifon was a space pilot as you know. He says that this Globe will make the journey as well as the one that was crushed. It is stocked with oxygen and has food and water machines. We can leave as soon as we like.'

Forgetting her father's injured arm Susan gave him a hug which made him wince.

'We're going home, we're going home,' she chanted.

Half an hour later sections of the tower roof peeled back like petals and through the aperture rose the Globe. For a moment it hung above the city while its computer set the course, then it began its eight hundred million mile journey Earthwards.

17 The Jasper Suggs Puzzle

When Roger opened his eyes he could hear Neerak saying, 'We will be landing at the New Zealand Time Pyramid in about an hour.'

Already the Globe was slowing so it would be able to drift down through the Earth's atmosphere without over-heating.

'I hope the Ronsons haven't been sending out search parties for us,' said Susan. 'I've no idea how long we have been away from the Awapuni Ranges.'

'It'll be overlooked when the wonders of the Pyramid become known,' said the Professor. Think what it'll mean to the world. With Atlaan knowledge it will become a paradise . . .'

'Simon,' said Neerak quietly, 'Gifon and I have come to a decision. The Time Pyramid must remain secret. We shall disappear once we have landed you safely.'

'You can't mean that, Neerak,' Professor White said. 'Your people expected you to pass on their knowledge. It would be a crime to deprive the human race of Aerial Globes, healing machines, time travel . . .'

Neerak shook her head.

'Your world is not ready for us. When Gifon recovered in his pyramid he tried to find out what sort of a world he had entered.'

'But he couldn't have found out much in the Antarctic,' Susan objected.

'It was easy for him to obtain an idea,' Neerak

replied. 'With equipment in the pyramid he was able to tune in on what you call "television" from all over the world. It gave him a view of life on Earth today, and what a terrible picture it was. Everywhere Man is fighting his brother. Sometimes it is open war, sometimes it is in secret with cowardly bombs, but the effect is the same – precious life is destroyed. Men despise each other for no other reason than the colouring of their skins, and in many countries men and women are imprisoned because they refuse to think the way their leaders tell them. Starvation is spreading across the Earth, yet the most advanced nations spend incredible amounts of money on the same weapons which brought disaster to the Atlaans.'

'But you have only seen the worst.' protested the Professor. 'There are good people in the world, there are good governments. The United Nations works for peace.'

'Of course there are good people,' said Neerak. 'You are good people, but if our secrets were revealed they would be used in bad ways by those who want power for themselves. You cannot give machines to children, they only hurt themselves, and until people have grown up our technology must remain hidden.'

'But your science would make us grow up.'

'No, your own discoveries have not made you peaceful. Have flying machines brought peace? Did your discovery of atomic power bring peace? I am afraid that nothing you can say will change our minds.'

The Professor said nothing. Susan thought for a while and then said: 'I think you're right.'

'What I said does not apply to you,' said Neerak in a softer voice. 'You are kind and brave and Gifon and I, wherever we reawaken, will never forget you.'

'What are you going to do?' asked Roger.

'After we have landed you, we will fly to the Antarctic Pyramid. There we shall go back into trance until we awake together in an age which can accept the

132

knowledge which was entrusted to us.'

An hour later the Globe came to rest gently on the slope near the summit of the *tapu* mountain, the same slope on which the children had seen the Mist Lizard. It was a hot South Pacific night and low over the horizon the Southern Cross blazed in the velvet sky.

'Farewell,' Gifon said solemnly.

To his surprise – and annoyance – Roger found that he was close to tears. Being a girl Susan could be more honest and she let her tears roll down her cheek. Silently they shook hands, then very quickly the two Atlaans sealed the Globe and seconds later it soared skywards. Soon afterwards the ground began to tremble.

* * *

Roger sat in his bedroom at his home in Harrow, working on a model of a Saturn rocket which he had begun some time before he had gone out to New Zealand with his uncle and Susan. He had returned to England sooner than had been expected with the result that his mother and father were away on holiday. In a way he was relieved because he was still too close to his adventures. He knew that if he talked about Mist Lizards, Time Pyramids and Cones they would think he was either mad or a dreadful liar – he did not have a scrap of evidence to prove anything that had happened to him.

Every trace of Neerak's pyramid had vanished from the mountain. Perhaps the Plaax with which it had been constructed had dissolved into atoms. At times he even wondered whether it had been a dream, a dream shared in some inexplicable way by Susan and her father. Strangely, now that it was all over, they seemed reluctant to talk about it.

Roger heard the front door bang as Susan came in. She and her father had been staying with Roger since they all arrived back at Heathrow Airport.

'I've got a nice postcard to send to Mani Potaka,' she called up the stairs. 'Come down and sign this card, it should be from both of us.'

He went down and was soon enjoying the adventures of Dougal as much as his cousin.

'Daddy and I are leaving tomorrow,' Susan said. 'He's hired a car and we're going to visit Mummy. . .'

Her eyes shone with pleasure at the thought.

'That's great,' Roger said. 'I hope it works out.'

'After that he's going on a dig at the Roman Wall so he won't be so far away this time.'

'I don't expect he'll find anything very exciting there – not like in New Zealand. I only wish I had something to tell me it was real – even a photograph of a pterodactyl would do.'

'I know what you mean,' said Susan. 'Can you keep a secret, Roger?'

He grinned.

'Risk telling me,'

'Look then.' Susan took out a little purse from the pocket of her jeans. She opened it and held something out to Roger, something that seemed to create its own light which it flashed in brilliant sparks.

'Why, that's Neerak's ring.'

'Yes, she slipped it to me when she said goodbye. Gifon had given it to her in her own time, but she whispered to me that she did not need it any more now that she was with him again.'

Roger held the flashing jewel and felt rather sad that he had no souvenir. Susan took it back quickly.

'That must be Daddy. He doesn't know about this. Being an archaeologist he might want to put it in a museum somewhere. I'll go and make him a cup of tea.'

The door chimes sounded again and Roger went to let the burly professor in. He carried a long parcel under his arm.

'Hello, Susie. Hello, Roger. I've got something rather interesting to show you.'

They went into the living-room and after Susan brought in tea he opened his wallet and took out a piece of paper. 'I spent the day at the Colindale Newspaper Library,' he said. 'They keep copies of every newspaper that's ever been published there. I wanted to check on a news item I remember reading as a boy. It was one of those silly little things which for some reason or other always stick in your mind. It took a while to find it, but here it is as I copied it from the *Daily Graphic*. It appeared in forty years ago.'

Roger took the paper and saw the heading AN EXTRAORDINARY THEFT. Under it was written: 'Fairground proprietor Jasper Suggs claimed this morning that he was the victim of an unusual theft. When he went to the site of his roundabout outside the village of Penmym he found that it had disappeared.

'The whole caboodle had just vanished as though it has been spirited away,' he told our reporter. 'All that was left were marks on the grass. It seems impossible that thieves could have dismantled a complete roundabout in the night and got away with it.'

'The local police are making enquiries but so far can shed no light on the theft. People of the village are inclined to believe it was Cornish piskies.'

'It intrigued me as a kid that a complete merry-go-round could vanish,' said the Professor. 'But I think we found the answer.'

'But what can it mean?' asked Roger.

'I'm not quite certain,' admitted his uncle. 'I think it got mixed up in the robots' time experiments. Somehow they accidentally caught the roundabout when they were trying out their time projector, and they mounted it in the city as a sort of monument to their achievement . . .'

'You mean it was snatched through time?'

'Something like that. Now. Roger, I've remembered that you will be fifteen next week so, as I won't be here, I'm going to give you your present now. Many happy returns.'

'Thank you, uncle. May I open it?' said Roger taking the long parcel.

'Of course.'

With Susan looking on excitedly Roger tore off the brown paper and found a strong cardboard box. He opened this carefully and gave a whoop of delight

'An astronomical telescope,' he cried. 'What a wonderful present'

'It's only a small one but I was assured that you will be able to see Saturn through it. I thought you might like that'

'It's getting dark already. I'll set it up in the garden and we can try it out.'

Susan and her father came out and watched while he fitted the telescope on its tripod and pointed it at the sky.

'I'll have to get a star map so I'll be able to locate Saturn,' Roger said. 'It's amazing to think that a few days ago we were up there, in that city which will stay on Titan for eternity.'

'Yes,' said the Professor, absent-mindedly rubbing his left arm.

That's more than can be said for the Time Pyramids,' Susan added thoughtfully. 'I wonder what has happened to them.'

'I think they have moved through time away from our age. We know the New Zealand one vanished, and I am sure that if we took an expedition to Antarctica we would find that one had gone too.'

'Backwards or forwards?' asked Susan.

Roger swivelled his telescope to where the moon was rising above Harrow Hill.

'Forwards of course,' he said. 'Neerak and Gifon have come from the past so obviously they will want to go on into the future to an age more suitable for them.'

'The twenty first century is very like that age Neerak told us about.' said Susan, 'when the people were wasting the Earth's resources and fighting each other. No wonder they did not want to stay here.'

'But we are in that age,' her father said quietly. The children looked at him puzzled.

'Don't you see? When they realized where they were they could not stay. This is the Age of Waste . . .'

'But if they came from the distant past . . .' began Roger.

'Yes, they've been coming forward not backwards,' Susan said.

'We only assumed that when we found the Pyramid,' said the Professor. 'And I am sure that Neerak thought so too, at first Perhaps she got an inkling of the truth when she talked to us, or as a result of Gifon watching television. But once they guessed the secret they realized they could not remain in our time.'

'But what secret?' demanded Susan.

'The Atlaan scientists realized after the nuclear war with the robots that atomic radiation would spread over the Earth until all life would be destroyed – so there was no point in bequeathing their knowledge to a dead world. They kept this terrible truth from the Sleepers, for they saw that the only chance for mankind was to try and change the course of history – to project the Sleepers *back* through the ages in the hope that somewhere, somehow, they would alter the sequence of events . . . for the better.'

'You mean . . .' began Roger, with a look of sudden understanding.

'Yes. Neerak and Gifon came from the future.'

—ooOoo—

137